MW00629020

Sailing with the Wind of Freedom:

Lascarina Bouboulis and the War for Greek Independence

By
KATHERINE KAYE

Illustrated by
DMITRI ANDREYEV

Sailing with the Wind of Freedom:
Lascarina Bouboulis and the War for Greek Independence

By Katherine Kaye
Illustrated by Dmitri Andreyev

Text and illustrations © 2023 Katherine Kaye
https://www.the-wind-of-freedom.com

Editor: Brett Peruzzi

Book Design/Art Direction: Levine Design
www.levinedesign.net

All rights reserved. No part of this book may be used or reproduced by any means, graphic, electronic or mechanical, including photocopying, recording or taping, or by any information storage retrieval systems without the express written permission of the author.

Library of Congress Control Number: 2022917476
ISBN: 9781941573389 (hardcover)
ISBN: 9781941573396 (paperback)

Published by Damianos Publishing
2 Central Street, Studio #152
Framingham, MA 01701 USA
www.DamianosPublishing.com

Produced through Silver Street Media
by Bridgeport National Bindery,
Agawam, MA USA

First printed 2023

Lascarina Lazarou has kept tongues on the Greek island of Spetses wagging for all fifteen years of her life. No one in the village knows who her father is, and Lascarina's mother takes care to guard this secret even from her own daughter. Worse yet, Lascarina herself has brought down on her head the disapproval of the islanders, as she possesses skills considered highly improper for a girl: she is a brilliant sailor and can read and write.

But the gossip that swirls around her and her family increases tenfold when she competes in the annual Saint Nicholas Day sailing race. The lessons she learns in that hard-fought competition will stand her in good stead all her life. In addition, she discovers that, for one young man with an independent mind, a troublesome reputation is no obstacle to friendship.

Lascarina Lazarou passes into history with the name Bouboulina. She brings the battle for freedom to the door of the Sultan's palace, winning help from a highly unlikely ally to whom she makes a fateful promise. She joins a secret society that unites the Greek people against the Ottoman Turks, who have occupied their lands for nearly 350 years. Using her own fortune, she builds a fleet of warships and in 1821 leads them into the first naval battle of the Greek War for Independence. But with the Sultan amassing all his forces against them, on land as well as sea, the Greeks stand to be crushed. Can Bouboulina save the Revolution?

In memory of my grandmother,
Vassiliki Liarou Giannakopoulos,
and my parents,
Georgia and Peter Kaye

Contents

The Ottoman Empire at the Time of the Greek War for Independence

Russia

England

France

Paris
Le Havre
Marseille

Gibraltar

Algeria

Venice

Lyons

Black Sea

Constantinople

Odessa

Aegean Sea

Crete

Peloponnesus

Mediterranean Sea

Alexandria

Key

Not Ottoman Territory

Ottoman Empire

Seas and Oceans

Peloponnesus

Patras
Tripolitsa
Spetses
Argos
Nauplion

Mani

Monemvasia

Prologue

In the late eighteenth and early nineteenth centuries, the old political order crumbled all across America and Europe. Colonies broke free of their mother countries and kings were toppled. At the same time, artists and poets glorified ancient Greece. The struggle for Greek independence reflected the ideals of its age.

When this story opens, Greece was part of the huge Ottoman Turkish Empire—and had been for nearly three hundred and fifty years. The Greek War for Independence was just one in a long series of revolts by the Greeks against their Ottoman overlords. Ever since the fall of their Byzantine Empire to the Turks in 1453, the Greeks had dreamed of regaining their freedom, remembering that the last Greek emperor had died without surrendering to the Ottomans.

Although this book is fictional, its heroine, Lascarina Bouboulis, did inspire the Greeks to prepare for war and led them in battle. She spent her large fortune building a Greek navy, passed into history as "Bouboulina," and was given the title "Admiral" by both Greeks and Russians. What we know of her life suggests that she possessed immense courage and intelligence—and a spirit that remained unbroken despite great personal and financial losses. Instead of providing a factual account of the Greek Revolution or a biography of Bouboulina, this novel leads you, reader, to a place that may seem exotic, and to a time in that place when women had little if any role in public life. It shows how one young woman who was willing to challenge the conventions of her society shaped her country's destiny as well as her own.

Characters in the Story

Main Characters - Greek/Russian

Lascarina Lazarou – our heroine, later known as Bouboulina, the Capitanissa

Paraskevi – Lascarina's mother

Captain Lazarou – Lascarina's stepfather

Ioannis – Paraskevi's brother, therefore Lascarina's uncle

Nicholas – Lascarina's half-brother

Soula – Lascarina's best friend

Dimitri Bouboulis – a successful young sea captain

Theodoros Kolokotronis – became general of the Greek Revolutionary Army, and known as the Old Man of the Mountains

Petrobey Mavromichaelis – powerful commander of warriors from Mani

Stavrianos Pinotsis – Lascarina's father

Harry – Captain Bouboulis's first mate

Yiannis, Georgios, Eleni – Bouboulina's children

Alexander Hypsilantis – very wealthy Greek who was also a prince at the Russian Court

Dimitri Hypsilantis – nephew of Alexander, Russian general who became leader of all Greek Revolutionary forces

Patriarch Grigorius – leader of the Orthodox Church

Stroganov – Russian ambassador to the Ottoman court

Father Constantinou – priest in Constantinople

Captain Miaoulis – naval commander from Hydra

Captain Kanaris – naval commander from Psara

Main Characters - Ottoman

Bey of Hydra – Ottoman Governor of the Saronic islands, occupied a fortress on Hydra

Mustafa – Ottoman tax collector on Spetses

Ali Pasha – vassal of the Sultan who ruled over Epirus

Sultan Mahmud – ruler of the Ottoman Empire at the time of the Greek Revolution

Valide Sultan Nakshidil – mother of the Sultan

Other Characters - Greek

Popi – the cobbler's daughter

Marika – Lascarina's half-sister

Captain Stenohori – wealthy captain who lived on Hydra with his family

Beka – a young Roma musician

Chrysophilos – merchant in Constantinople

Captain Solaris – friend of Captain Lazarou, from Spetses

Father Spiros – priest and teacher on Spetses

Father Andreas – successor to Father Spiros

Captain Stamos – friend of Dimitri Bouboulis, from Spetses

Peter – young boy on Spetses

Delos – captain from Hydra

Captain Apostolis – sea captain from Psara

Bishop Germanos – Revolutionary leader from Patras

Captain Istianou – captain from Constantinople

Captain Lefkarou – captain from Spetses

Lykos – Greek ruffian

Panos – son of General Kolokotronis

Other Characters - Ottoman

Ahmad – Secretary to the Ottoman Minster of Finance

Rahman – Ottoman Minster of Finance

Alev – harem slave

General Dramali – Ottoman General charged by the Sultan to crush the Greek Revolution

Murad-Ali – Kaptan Pasha or admiral of Ottoman navy

I

A Secret on Spetses

Under the bright morning sun, the island of Spetses sparkled like an emerald in the turquoise Aegean Sea. It was 1786. Across Europe, streets and drawing rooms alike buzzed with talk of the overthrow of the British king by the American colonists and of revolution brewing in France. But Spetses slept, along with the rest of what once was Greece—or so hoped the Ottoman Turks, who had occupied these lands since 1453. They knew better than to let down their guard, though, for they had learned that even the soundest slumber could be disturbed by fitful dreams— of freedom. Only twenty years earlier, this island had seethed with rebellion.

Fifteen-year-old Lascarina Lazarou stepped briskly down a narrow path through Spetses's thick pine forest. Like other islanders, her family lived in fear of pirate raids and had built their home away from the shore, far up one of the island's many hills. Lascarina carried a man's pair of worn-out shoes.

She paused at her favorite point along the path and squinted at the left side of the harbor, where her sailboat—the *Dolphin*—bobbed at its mooring, jib and mainsail furled. Five years ago, her stepfather unloaded this small, graceful sloop from his ship and said it was for Lascarina. The villagers at once wagged their tongues with disapproval: sailing was an unacceptable activity for a girl, they said firmly. Captain Lazarou smiled and paid them no mind: he started teaching his stepdaughter how to sail the boat the very day he delivered it. Now, though, Lascarina had little time for sailing. She had to help her mother look after four younger half-brothers and sisters.

Remembering her mother's admonition to "look present-able," Lascarina quickly braided her waist-long wavy chestnut hair and brushed off twigs that clung to her ankle-length skirt and apron. Her clothes hung loosely on her tall, thin frame. She was well aware that people thought her plain: her large eyes were an odd shade of gray, her nose was too bony, and her mouth too broad. Still, she fastened the silver buttons of her short wool jacket and laced her leather boots, which revealed her to be from a family of traders rather than farmers.

At this time of day, the village bustled with carts drawn by horses and donkeys. The tangy smell of fresh fish still hung in the salty air, left over from the catch hauled in and sold by fishermen earlier in the morning. Two barques were in port; one belonged to her stepfather and the other to his friend, Captain Solaris. Both had recently returned from voyages across the Mediterranean Sea, to Italy and France. Lascarina gazed at them for a moment, listening to the waves lap against their hulls. Then she turned right along the village's freshly cobbled main street.

Just fifteen years ago, around the time of her birth, this village had been a pile of charred rubble. By now, though, new stucco buildings had risen out of the ashes. Their orange-tiled roofs and whitewashed walls shone in the strong sunlight. Most of these buildings housed the offices of shipping companies, for Spetses's captains had rebuilt their firms and regained their renown as able sailors and shrewd businessmen. Down a bit further was the island's shipyard: Lascarina inhaled the scent of freshly sawed pine and again paused to admire the wooden frame of a sloop just emerging from the yard. Next, she passed the island's one inn and taverna, frequented by visiting captains and sailors, and the marketplace, where two days each week, villagers milled around the stalls of farmers and merchants. Finally, she reached the shops of the tradesmen who served the islanders—the smith, the weaver, and the cobbler.

It was this last shop that Lascarina entered, hoping not to encounter the shoemaker's oldest daughter. No such luck. There was Popi, slouched against the counter, caught up in conversation with another teenage girl. Both wore dresses of homespun cotton, but cut in what they imagined to be the latest French style, with tight bodices.

"You mean that he's breaking their engagement?" Popi asked her friend excitedly, her small, beady eyes sparkling with malicious delight. "Her reputation will be ruined!"

Then she caught sight of Lascarina. "Well, speaking of reputations…" she crowed. "Look who's here! Spetses's famous lady sailor."

Lascarina braced herself. Already she could feel her palms start to sweat. She set the shoes on the counter. "The soles need repair. Captain Lazarou would like them back next week."

"Right, Captain Lazarou, your *step*-father," said Popi scornfully.

Lascarina knew what was coming: always the same taunt.

"I don't suppose you've found out who your *real* father is?" asked Popi.

"You asked me the exact same question four weeks ago, if you recall," said Lascarina drily. "No, I haven't learned anything new since then."

Popi's pasty complexion reddened, and her thick features contorted with anger and resentment. Who did Lascarina think she was, speaking in such a superior tone? "You think you're so swell with your fine leather boots and silver buttons!" she hissed. "You're nothing but the daughter of a hussy who snagged herself a decent husband."

With this, Lascarina took a deep breath. "You have no right to slander my mother," she said, trembling with rage. But as she looked at Popi, so stupid, so hopeless, she also felt a twinge of something like pity. "Look," she continued, "I've told you…"

"Oh, we *know*," interrupted Popi. " *'My father was an honorable man,' "* she squealed in a high-pitched voice. "We've heard it a hundred times. Is that why your rich relatives from Hydra abandoned your mother here?" Popi and her friend burst into shrill laughter that brought the cobbler running into the shop.

"Popi, that's enough," he said sternly. "Go home and help your mother."

Lascarina looked at him gratefully and left on the counter a silver coin, a Turkish *akce*, to pay for the repair. Popi, stung by her father's reprimand, took her friend by the arm and flounced out of the shop. At the door, though, she turned and snarled to Lascarina, "All right, sailor girl. Maybe your real father was some great captain. Why don't you make your family proud? Enter the Saint Nicholas Day Race, and show us how well you can sail against the boys!"

Two old village women—who had overheard this exchange—entered the shop, their black scarves covering gray hair pulled tightly back from their faces. Lascarina took the opportunity to flee, heading in the direction opposite to Popi.

The embarrassed cobbler turned to the two women. "I don't know why Popi acts like that," he said wearily. "Surely, if there had been any disgrace around Lascarina's mother, Paraskevi, our good Captain Lazarou would never have married her."

One of the women bobbed her head. "Yes," she said, "We all know how brave Captain Lazarou is; he rescued Captain Solaris and then hid with him from the Turks for two years after our men were defeated. Still, you have to admit that Lascarina *is* a tomboy. What else would you expect when her mother sends her to school and allows her to sail?"

"I remember the day Paraskevi arrived on Spetses," said her friend, "newborn baby in arms, with a man who *claimed* to be her brother. Our friend Mustafa…"—the two others groaned, for Mustafa was the Turkish tax collector—"…occupied the only building left standing. Paraskevi and the man rushed over to him and showed him the deed to some land up the hill that their family had owned for centuries—they had never paid attention to it, didn't even rent it out. The man helped Paraskevi clean a ramshackle cottage up there and cleared a small farm for her. Then he went back to Hydra, returning just two or three times each year to help her. It's very strange. Paraskevi has been tight-lipped about all this, even to this day. But I don't think there's any scandal around Paraskevi," she said firmly. "You know, those high-born folks from Hydra have different ways."

Although Hydra was just the next island over in the Saronic Gulf, it was a world apart from Spetses. Most of its wealthy merchant families had refrained from participating in the ill-fated Orloff Rebellion of 1771. The Spetsiotes, on the other hand, had taken up arms. Sea captains and farmers together battled the Turks, helped at first by their powerful Russian allies. But the Russians soon abandoned the struggle, and the rebellion failed. Ottoman brigades overran Spetses, burning the harbor town and slaughtering any inhabitants who had remained there. After delivering this lesson to the rebels, the Turkish soldiers decamped to more hospitable Hydra, leaving behind only Mustafa, who once each year descended upon every Spetsiote household to take a census and collect the tribute due the Ottoman Sultan.

Unaware of the conversation in the village, Paraskevi worked with her servant at the big stone oven in the courtyard of her home to prepare the family's dinner. Her hair, still dark brown, was pulled into a neat bun. From her early years tending the farm, her skin, once so white, had become tawny. She wondered what was keeping her oldest daughter and walked to the front of the house. Her deep-set dark eyes, gray as Lascarina's, scanned the horizon. Suddenly she spied her daughter rushing up the path. With one glance at her tear-stained face, Paraskevi guessed what had happened.

Lascarina burst through the gate. "Why can't you just tell me who my father is? *Now!*" she shouted.

"Lascarina, you must ignore those fools," said Paraskevi gently. "Please believe me—it is for your own safety that we keep the truth from you. Someday, you will know who your father was."

"You say the same thing every time this happens. When will that day come?"

Lascarina knew her mother would not answer. She ran up the stairs to the room she shared with her half-sister, threw herself on the bed, and pulled a woven blanket over her head. Not even the aroma of grilled fish could entice her to the table.

While the four younger children chattered amongst themselves, Paraskevi told Captain Lazarou how Lascarina had been taunted. A frown creased his forehead, and his usually good-natured blue eyes darkened. "That girl, Popi, has her brain— small as it is—in the gutter. It's hard to believe that any villager would think twice about the rubbish she spews," he said. "Why don't we just tell Lascarina the truth about her father?"

"No," said Paraskevi quickly. "You know that if she is provoked, she will not be able to keep this secret to herself, at least not yet."

"Do you really think that if Mustafa found out, he would report us to the Governor on Hydra?"

"Maybe," murmured Paraskevi, "if there is still a price on my head. Of course, we can always bribe Mustafa. It's our neighbors who worry me. They might just talk to the *Bey's* officers to try to verify the story."

Lazarou sighed and nodded his head in agreement. He walked over to the stairs. "Hey, where's my favorite sailor?" he called.

Lascarina came down the stairs and tried to smile, but Lazarou saw her puffy eyes. "Won't you come to dinner? I brought home a sea bass, your favorite."

"Thank you," said Lascarina. "I don't think I could do the fish justice tonight."

"Lascarina," he said. "everywhere, in cities and villages, you will find some folks who are just too stupid and mean to do anything but gossip. Try to be patient."

"I will," she said, coming to the table to hug her younger brothers and sisters.

"Lascarina, we missed you!" said Nicholas, the oldest of her half-siblings.

"Missed you too," she said. "And Mama, I'm sorry; I know this is not your fault."

Paraskevi came to her and took her hand. "My brave daughter, you are more like your father than you will ever know. Sleep well."

Race!

Lascarina tossed in her bed through the night. Could there be a shred of truth to what Popi had said? Could her father have been anything other than honorable? Could he have been a *criminal*? Was he for sure dead? Had he abandoned his wife and daughter and disappeared? No, she thought. Her mother could not have remarried if her father was still alive, and Paraskevi would not lie: not telling the full story was far different from lying.

Lascarina reached as far back as she could for the earliest memories from her childhood. She could see herself as a toddler, playing in the garden of the small cottage that Paraskevi and Uncle Ioannis had cleaned up, the cottage that Lazarou had built into the fine house they lived in now. She remembered Uncle Ioannis visiting them, bouncing her on his knees, and talking about her grandparents and cousins on Hydra… and then, one day a couple of years later, bringing Captain Lazarou to meet her mother. After that, Lazarou would stop by to see Paraskevi between his voyages. Lascarina liked this good-natured captain, who took the time to walk her down to the dock and show her his ships. With a drowsy smile, she recalled how she scrambled up the rigging of Lazarou's largest brig. The crew could not find her and the distraught captain thought she had fallen overboard until, finally, a sailor spotted her and climbed up to rescue her.

And shortly after that came her first voyage to the neighboring island of Hydra—Lazarou and Paraskevi had decided to marry there. Lascarina remembered being smothered in the embrace of her grandparents as soon as she stepped off the ship, then hustled off to a tiny chapel where Uncle Ioannis and the families of her mother's sister and older brother waited. After the service, they left the chapel quietly, inconspicuously, in small groups, and met at her grandparents' home for a feast. To Lascarina then, that home seemed like a mansion: it had two stories, a courtyard, timbered balconies, fine furniture, leather-bound books on the shelves, and even paintings on the walls. Paraskevi and Lazarou left her with her grandparents while they sailed to Venice for a short wedding trip. Lascarina thought about how puzzled and hurt she felt when her grandparents warned her to tell no one that she was their granddaughter, and how her grandmother's hands trembled when they encountered the Ottoman *Bey* on one of their strolls and she told him that her young guest was the daughter of a distant cousin. As soon as Captain Lazarou and Paraskevi returned with her to Spetses, the Captain enlarged their cottage. Just in time, thought Lascarina, as a new baby arrived in each of the next four years. Whenever she remembered her stay with her grandparents, she felt grateful to live on Spetses, away from the fear that had surrounded her on Hydra.

So Lascarina was astonished to learn, the day her sailboat was delivered, that it was her mother's parents—her reserved, careful grandparents—who had designed every detail of the sloop. They even sent Uncle Ioannis to find out from Lazarou her thoughts about figureheads! The sloop was built to their specifications in one of Hydra's shipyards, with a blue dolphin at its prow—and the *Bey* was told that Captain Lazarou would be delivering it to her grandfather's business partner. At first, Paraskevi objected strenuously to these proceedings, but slowly Ioannis convinced her that all would be well. Lascarina learned quickly how to sail: by the time she was eleven, she was allowed to take the *Dolphin* out on her own. All her life she remembered how her distant grandparents had seen so clearly into her heart.

Finally, she drifted off to sleep.

She woke at daybreak and padded across the cool, smooth wooden floor planks to her window. Popi's taunt flashed into her mind as she gazed at the lightening sea: *Maybe your real father was some great captain. Why don't you make your family proud? Enter the Saint Nicholas Day Race, and show us how well you can sail against the boys!* The words echoed in her ears.

"*That* I can do," thought Lascarina, "no matter who my father was."

She reasoned with herself: "But what good would it do? It would just create more food for gossip!"

The sun rose higher on the horizon, its rosy gold light reflected in the sea. "Never mind," she thought. "It will show the villagers that sailing is in my blood, something I inherited from this unknown father of mine."

The feast day of Saint Nicholas, patron of sailors and fishermen, fell on December 6. Every year on that day, the island's best sailors competed in a race along Spetses's southern coast.

In years past, Lascarina had gathered with the villagers to watch the race from the cliffs of one of the island's hills. This year, she resolved, she would enter it herself.

She would need the help of her best friend, Soula, the oldest daughter of the farmer who owned the land next to her family's. Later that morning, as Soula brought her goats to pasture, Lascarina caught up with her.

"Wait!" called Lascarina across the field. "I need to talk to you."

Soula walked over, her loose homespun dress fluttering in the breeze and her goats scampering along the path they knew well. Wisps of sun-bleached hair escaped from her kerchief. She greeted her friend with a broad smile: "What's up?"

Lascarina told her about what had happened in the village and her decision to compete in the Saint Nicholas Day Race herself. Soula's smile faded. "Lascarina," she said, "you've heard this slander so many times before. Just what do you intend to prove now by doing this?"

"That women can sail as well as men," laughed Lascarina. "It took Popi to put *that* idea into my head." Then, becoming more serious, she said, "Soula, I just cannot keep replying to their taunts with the same old answer. If I win this race, these people will see that I have something in me that their words cannot crush, something I got from my father."

"But you yourself have always wanted to know who he was," said Soula softly.

"Yes, and someday—I don't know when—my mother and Lazarou will tell me."

"Lascarina," said Soula patiently, "the judges will not even let you *enter* the race."

"I know. I will not join the others at the lineup. There's a small cove about two hundred yards from there. You can't see it from where the judges and viewers stand. I'm going to hide the *Dolphin* and begin from there when the starting shot is fired. Once the race is on, no one will be able to stop me."

"But you'll handicap yourself."

"It won't be hard to catch up with the others. I know those waters well. Besides, there's no other way. There's only one week left to the race. Will you help me?"

Soula's light brown eyes were clouded with worry. If Lascarina lost, she would be the laughingstock of Spetses. But Soula had sailed with her friend many times. She knew that Lascarina would not lose. No creature but a sea hawk could predict changes in the wind as fast and unerringly as her friend. Moreover, this was no harebrained scheme; Lascarina had planned every detail.

Soula's eyes brightened again. In a firm voice, she said, "All right. What do I need to do?"

Lascarina hugged her. "I was sure you'd say that!" she exclaimed, pulling out a long length of thick rope from under her jacket. "So sure that I brought along some rope for you to learn how to make a sailor's knot. Next Tuesday, the day before the race, I will sail the *Dolphin* at the crack of dawn over to the cove. You must meet me there to help me moor the boat. I will toss you the rope—you have to catch it, or we will have a problem. You'll need to tie it to a tree—there are a lot around there—and I will wade to shore. The next day, the day of the race, you must meet me there to untie the boat so that I can cast off."

"Exactly where is this cove?" asked Soula.

Lascarina explained which path Soula needed to follow to reach the small inlet.

"Hmm. If I, um, borrow my father's horse," said Soula, "I can be down there and back again by the time everyone at the farm is up and about."

"Good. Now, *this* is the type of knot you need to tie." Lascarina showed Soula how to tie a square knot, and Soula practiced with the rope. "You will need to pull hard."

Once Soula mastered the square knot, the girls parted.

On each of the next few days, Lascarina finished her chores early so that she could check the *Dolphin's* rigging, scrub the deck and add a fresh coat of blue paint to the figurehead. She remembered that dolphins are said to befriend ship-wrecked sailors.

At the cock's first crow on Tuesday morning, Lascarina was up. Noiselessly she dressed and crept down the stairs to the granary, where she hid an extra set of clothing. The only others about at this time of day were the fishermen. So that none would see her, she walked down to the *Dolphin* along a little-used forest path.

As soon as the first thin rays of winter sunlight fell on the calm sea, she set out. The weak morning breeze seemed to shift direction every five minutes, and Lascarina had to adjust her jib often to make good time. Finally, she spotted the cove and waved to Soula, who was pacing the shore. Lascarina proceeded slowly, taking care not to scrape the *Dolphin* on any rocks. She rolled up her mainsail and jib and paddled the sailboat closer to shore.

The sun was just over the horizon. Lascarina called, "Here, Soula, catch!" With all her strength, she heaved to the shore a heavy coil of rope, which was tied to an iron loop in the deck. It landed just at the water's edge. Soula dashed to pick it up before a wave pulled it back into the sea. Quickly she found the nearest tree and knotted the rope around its trunk. Lascarina lowered herself into the chilly waist-deep water and walked to the shore. She checked the knot that Soula had tied. It was secure. The girls ran to the old plow horse that Soula had tethered to a tree near the path.

Soula glanced at the sky. "It's at least seven-thirty—we have to hurry," she said. With both girls on his back, the horse refused to move.

"This will never do," said Lascarina, dismounting. "I'll walk. Can you meet me here at eleven tomorrow morning?"

"Yes. I'll get my work done early and make up some excuse to go to the village." Soula waved, and the horse plodded back to the farm.

Lascarina ran along the quiet path to the granary, quickly changed into her dry clothes, and hid her wet dress until she could hang it somewhere. The scent of freshly baked bread wafted over from the courtyard's stone oven as she joined her family at the roughhewn table of pine planks where they took their morning meal.

"Lascarina!" cried little Marika, the half-sister who shared her room. "Where were you this morning? I didn't see you and I got scared. And there was no one to help me with my clothes."

For a second, Lascarina froze. Then, she hugged the little girl. "Marika, I am so sorry. I forgot that I had promised to talk to Soula. But see, you did a good job dressing yourself."

Paraskevi glanced sharply at Lascarina. "You look flushed," she said. "Are you feeling well?"

"Yes," said Lascarina. But she was so nervous that, despite her hunger, she could eat only a few bites. She glanced at the sky at least every ten minutes, trying to fathom tomorrow's weather, planning sailing strategies for every combination of winds she could imagine. She was glad to sit with her embroidery that afternoon. Most villagers would have been surprised to learn that Lascarina Lazarou *liked* to embroider; counting out cross-stitch patterns and seeing the beautiful designs emerge on her canvas helped her clear her mind, to focus.

Again at dinner that evening, Lascarina's heart skipped a beat. Captain Lazarou said, "This afternoon, I chanced to walk past the pier where you keep the *Dolphin*. I didn't see it. What happened? Did it need another repair of some sort?"

"Yes," said Lascarina, "one of the deck boards had become loose. I could not fix it and sailed it over to *Barba* Yianni's. It's probably in the shipyard by now."

"All right," said Lazarou, "but next time, please tell me first so that I can see if I can repair it. *Barba* Yianni is getting too old for this kind of heavy carpentry."

Lascarina was alarmed at how easily a lie had slipped out of her lips and felt her throat tighten with guilt; she had never before deceived the Captain.

The next morning, at dawn, Lascarina peered outside her window. She murmured the old sailor's rhyme: "Red sun at night, sailors take delight; red sun in morning, sailors take warning." Those heavy orange clouds hanging on the horizon boded an overcast day.

All of her morning chores were finished before breakfast. "You're in such a frenzy," laughed the Captain, "that one would think you were entering the race yourself!"

"I thought I'd leave early, to choose good seats for us," Lascarina said.

"Not a good day for sailing," muttered Lazarou. "Try to find a place out of the wind."

Lascarina ran down the path to the cove and met Soula. The *Dolphin* was bobbing at its mooring, just as they had left it, a bright speck of blue against the lead-gray sea and sky. As soon as her friend climbed into the sloop, Soula untied the rope. Lascarina pulled it in and paddled to the mouth of the cove.

Still out of their sight, she could hear the noise of the crowd assembling on the cliffs above. Among the spectators were her worried parents. Where could the girl be? They knew she would not miss this race for the world. Lascarina unfurled her sail.

"Good luck!" shouted Soula, who tried to smile as she wiped her sweating palms on her apron.

"Thank you for everything!" Lascarina shouted back.

The starting shot was fired. She was off!

The breeze was light. It was a full ten minutes before Lascarina sailed into the spectators' view, trailing the rest of the boats by at least one hundred yards.

"What's *that*?" one of the judges asked. "That boat wasn't in the entry lineup. Some fisherman must have forgotten that we have the race today." Just then, a small puff of wind caused Lascarina's skirt to billow out. "Good God! It's a *woman*!"

Popi elbowed her way to the front of the crowd and was the first to recognize the mysterious racer. "It's Lascarina!" she cried. "Hah! I can't believe it! The fool took my dare—she's going to show us how well she can sail against the boys!"

Paraskevi buried her face, crimson with embarrassment, in her hands, but Captain Lazarou made his way to the cliff's edge. "Now I'll see if I was a good teacher," he said to himself, nervously.

Lascarina had never been more grateful for the *Dolphin's* lightness. A few maneuvers of the mainsail brought her to the middle of the flotilla. A steady Northeaster had blown up, and rain started to fall.

Lascarina changed her course to a dead run, sailing directly with the wind, squeezing the maximum amount of distance from every gust. She well knew that the smallest shift in the wind could cause the boom, the heavy cross beam from which the sail was hoisted, to swing about in a sudden jibe and knock her overboard—or tear a poorly set sail to shreds. The dead run was worth the risk, though, for she was catching up with the third boat from the lead. The spectators were dumbfounded. Captain Lazarou beamed with pride.

Lascarina kept a watchful eye on her telltale. As soon as she saw the ribbon flutter, she knew that the wind would change direction. In a flash, she loosened the boom and let it swing to the other side of the *Dolphin*.

The sailors of the second and third boats were not so quick. One was swept overboard by a sudden jibe; out of the corner of her eye, Lascarina could see him scrambling back onto his deck. The other was trying to roll up the fragments of his torn sail. Up on the cliff, everyone begged to take a look through the judges' telescope.

The *Dolphin* flew from one wave to the next, heeling all the way to the leeward side. Lascarina was drenched in the spray of the sea, but she did not feel cold. Her heart soared! She had overtaken the first boat. In a few minutes, she would be at the finish line. "Never again, Popi, will you ask me about my father," she shouted into the wind.

The wind grew stronger. A wave crashed onto her deck. She grabbed the side rail in the nick of time.

The sailor who trailed her was not so lucky. When Lascarina looked over her shoulder, she saw him bobbing in the water near his floundering boat. The finish line was only two hundred feet away. Lascarina could almost feel in her hands the silver cup that was awarded as first prize. For some reason, the roar of the crowd had ceased. Again she glanced behind her. Why was the sailor of the boat she had overtaken not yet back on deck? She squinted—and saw him flailing in the water, tangled in his lanyards!

"He could drown," she realized, horrified. From deep in her heart, a sob rose to her lips. Why did this have to happen when she was so close?

There was only one thing she could do. And there was no time to lose. With a breaking heart, she released her sail and tacked back to the unlucky sailor. When she was a few feet away from him, she let her sail go completely slack and used her oar as best she could in the pounding waves to paddle to the side of his boat.

"Grab this," she shouted, tossing out her rope.

The boy could barely muster the strength to hold on, so furiously had he been struggling in the sea. Lascarina pulled the rope in with all her might. She recognized her competitor as one of her classmates from Father Spiros's school. He looked at her in shock and gasped, "Lascarina!" As she helped him climb on to the Dolphin's deck, she saw one of the other boats sail past the finish line. Her old classmate followed the direction of her gaze. "I'm sorry this cost you the race," he coughed.

Lascarina tried hard to fight back her tears. She said nothing but sailed on, slowly and carefully now, feeling the salt in every one of her rope burns.

Waiting at the very head of the cheering crowd, which had descended to the shore, were the parents of the rescued sailor. Lascarina saw the gratitude in their eyes and knew that, even though the silver cup had been won by another, she would never again hear the villagers taunt her.

Then she felt herself in the embrace of her own parents. "I am sorry I lied to you," she whispered. "I hope you are not too angry."

"*Angry?*" The Captain was almost bouncing with joy. "I am about to burst with pride!"

Paraskevi pressed her lips together tightly to keep from smiling. "Well, Lascarina," she said, "you have given our neighbors an entirely new topic of conversation: this should busy their tongues for the next decade!"

The villagers lined up to congratulate her, shaking their heads. As much as they frowned upon her entering the race, they knew full well that one of the island boys would have drowned had she not been there. In their midst was a wiry young captain; though only twenty-two, he was already renowned as one of the Mediterranean's most daring merchants. He had lived in Spetses as a child and once won this race himself. Whenever he chanced to be back home in December, he made sure not to miss it.

"That was the best sailing I've ever seen!" he said, as he bowed to Lascarina. "My name is Dimitri Bouboulis. A few years ago, I sailed this race—but I did not face the challenges you had!"

Lascarina first looked at the ground and then mustered the courage to meet the young captain's friendly gaze. She noted that his face was deeply tanned and framed in black, curly hair—and that his dark brown eyes were full of admiration. She blushed, realizing that she had never taken such care to study a man's face before. "Thank you," she said.

Bouboulis left the shore with a few other captains and sailors. "Who is that young woman?" he asked.

"Lascarina?" said one. "She's Captain Lazarou's stepdaughter. Quite a character, don't you think?"

"Yes, she certainly *does* have character," murmured Bouboulis.

III

One People?

A few days after the race, Lascarina and her stepfather walked to the harbor and saw an impressive three-master being caulked at one of the docks.

"Is that the ship of Captain Bouboulis?" asked Lascarina.

"Yes." Lazarou looked at her with surprise. "How do you know Bouboulis?"

"He congratulated me."

"Oh, right," said Lazarou. "Yes, that is one of Bouboulis's. He keeps most of his ships up in Odessa, on the Black Sea—does a lot of business with the Ukrainians and Russians. This beauty, though, was built right in our own shipyard. It's the first time he's sailing her." His eyes wandered to the bowsprit where, in gold letters, was written the word *Elpida*—Hope. Lazarou smiled. "It's a wonder the Ottomans let him get away with that—I guess they read it as hope for surviving pirate attacks."

"And you think he means hope for Greek freedom?"

Lazarou nodded.

"Do you know where he's going?" continued Lascarina.

"Le Havre, far up the western coast of France."

"Why, that's well past Gibraltar! His barque looks strong enough—do you think he will make it past the Barbary pirates?"

Lazarou observed that Lascarina's eyes registered dismay. "He's survived enough scrapes with those vermin," he said. "But they *are* growing stronger—I've heard they're even menacing Ottoman ships."

That evening, after Lascarina had gone to bed, Lazarou said to Paraskevi, "I think our girl is smitten."

Lascarina's mother laughed. "With a ship?"

"With a shipowner—Captain Bouboulis."

Paraskevi raised her eyebrows. "Well, my daughter has high hopes—I hear only good things about that young man. But how does she even know his name?"

"Apparently Bouboulis congratulated her after the race."

Paraskevi and Lazarou looked at one another, sharing the same thought. "Where is he off to?" Paraskevi asked.

"Le Havre."

"Le Havre! He will be gone for months—perhaps he will not even return. You said yourself that the pirates from Algiers grow increasingly bold."

"Yes. I did not tell Lascarina about the capture of the ship from Hydra."

Paraskevi sighed. "Even if Bouboulis does make it back, it's best for Lascarina to forget about him. Wealthy fathers everywhere will be trying to catch him for their own daughters, luring him with huge dowries. His family surely will push him to make a good match."

"Oh, Paraskevi, you're always so practical. Let us daydream a bit."

Paraskevi frowned but said nothing.

"And besides," Lazarou continued thoughtfully, "Bouboulis has no family left now. His parents died in Odessa a few years ago, and so, sadly, did a younger sister."

"But I thought he grew up here," said Paraskevi.

"He lived here until he was fifteen, and then his family moved to Odessa to be closer to his mother's people. In any case," said Lazarou firmly, "I doubt very much that *that* young man would marry for gold."

Unaware that he was a topic of discussion in the Lazarou household, Dimitri Bouboulis sat that evening in his cabin on the *Elpida's* stern, reviewing his ledgers. He had been down in the hold all afternoon, checking the cargo he was carrying to Le Havre: barrels of olive oil from Kalamata, on the Greek mainland, and, for the new home of a wealthy nobleman near Paris, slabs of polished black marble from the quarries of Thassos, an island in the north Aegean Sea.

"Both will fetch a good price in Le Havre," he thought, "if I can just get there."

Dimitri was well aware that a captain from Hydra had been killed in a battle with the Barbary pirates near Gibraltar. The two cannons he carried on his ship—the maximum allowed by the Ottomans, who were ever fearful of letting their Greek subjects arm themselves—were no match for the pirates' brigantines, which bristled with cannons. In the hold of the *Elpida*, along with the cargo, were enough long guns and pistols for every one of his sailors to use, if necessary. Like all merchant captains, Dimitri had a warrant from the Ottoman Minister of Commerce that allowed him to carry these weapons only for the duration of the voyage; he would return them to the Turkish armory at Constantinople before setting foot again on Greek or Russian soil. Dimitri's face grew taut as he thought of his crew—twenty sailors recruited from Odessa, Constantinople, and the Saronic Islands, ranging in age from fifteen to fifty. "All able and willing to fight," he thought, "but how many have seen combat?"

Wanting to drive these worries from his mind, Captain Bouboulis strode out of his quarters, which suddenly seemed hot and stuffy. He took a brisk stroll on deck. His unease vanished as soon as he felt the cool, salty breeze on his face. He gazed at the masts of his newest ship, which had rolled out of Spetses's shipyard just two months ago. "Sturdy," he thought, "but light. The builders here know their business. I think we'll be all right."

His mind wandered to a narrow escape—from danger of a different sort. He grinned. The morning after the Saint Nicholas Day Race, he had borrowed a sloop from the shipyard and sailed to Hydra with only his first mate, Harry. He had been invited there by one of Hydra's captains to discuss a matter related to his forthcoming voyage—he thought. He found the captain's mansion and was ushered by a servant into the mahogany-paneled drawing room. Within a few moments, Captain Stenohori appeared, followed by two women, one rather stout, with graying hair drawn up into an elaborate pile on top of her head, the other no more than twenty, fair and quite pretty, her face surrounded by blond ringlets. Their elegantly cut silk dresses—surely from Paris, thought Dimitri—rustled softly as they moved. "Captain Bouboulis," beamed Stenohori, "welcome to my home. Let me introduce you to my wife and oldest daughter, Sophia."

Dimitri bowed. "It's so kind of you to invite me here to discuss the new rigging you mentioned. I really thought we would meet at the dock."

"Why, no problem at all, my boy. We know you are off to Le Havre soon. Before such a long and dangerous voyage, a little entertainment is in order."

"Yes, Captain Bouboulis," trilled Madame Stenohori with a stiff smile, "we've arranged a concert for you. Sophia has been studying harpsichord with Monsieur Laureche. We brought him back from Paris to instruct all our daughters. And we have a brand-new instrument from Vienna. So, please, *do* make yourself comfortable."

"Oh," said Dimitri, sinking into a well-stuffed side chair, "how lovely." Soon he was served some steaming tea—in a porcelain cup from France, he noted.

Sophia curtsied and warbled softly, "I will play Mozart's *Sonata in F Major.*"

Dimitri happened to love music and was familiar with Mozart's work, having attended many concerts in Odessa. The piece that Sophia was about to perform was written for a child.

Sophia played mechanically, squashing all lightness out of the sweet sonata. When she stood and bowed, she looked quite satisfied with herself. Dimitri cast about for something, anything, to say: "Why, Mademoiselle Stenohori, that was charming. You have just started your studies with Monsieur Laureche?"

Sophia looked at him with haughty disbelief. "Why I've been studying for three years!" she exclaimed sharply.

"Never mind, Sophia," said Madame Stenohori shrilly. "Go fetch your sister." She turned again to Dimitri: "Our second oldest studies singing…"

"Ah…How many daughters do you have?"

"Five," muttered Captain Stenohori, somewhat grimly.

A second silk-swathed daughter appeared, curtsied, and without so much as an introduction, launched into what Dimitri recognized, with difficulty, as a piece from *The Marriage of Figaro*. He bolted out of his chair. The singer, oblivious, continued. Captain Stenohori looked at Dimitri with concern. "What's the matter? My dear boy, are you ill?"

"Oh, forgive me, Captain, but I've just realized that I forgot to sign a contract with one of the merchants whose goods I am carrying. I have it in my cabin on the *Elpida*. I must return to Spetses immediately. Please convey my apologies to your wife and daughters. Charming, all, charming…"

Madame Stenohori bustled over to the men. "What's happening?" she asked.

Too late. Dimitri had reached the front door.

"You forgot your hat!"

But Dimitri was well on his way to the dock.

Madame Stenohori glared at her husband. "Those Spetsiotes just don't know how to behave in polite society." She interrupted herself to shout at her daughter: "Helen, you can stop singing!"

Turning back to her husband, she said, "You should never have invited him."

"Right as usual, my dear," said Captain Stenohori with resignation. He turned to his five crestfallen daughters, who, by this time, had all gathered in the drawing room. "Don't worry, darlings, with the dowry I'm prepared to bestow upon each of you, we'll have no trouble finding more suitable grooms."

Meanwhile, Dimitri bounded back on board the sloop. "Cast off, Harry!" he gasped to his bewildered first mate.

"But Captain, it's almost evening."

"Never mind! We're leaving *now*."

Dimitri returned to the present. His grin faded as he thought of the journey that lay ahead. The following morning, he rounded up Harry and his crew and set sail for Le Havre.

Over the next few months, Lascarina helped Paraskevi look after the younger children. At the same time, Captain Lazarou entrusted his stepdaughter with more and more of his book-keeping, having observed that she was good with numbers. She could also read as well as any boy on the island. Paraskevi may have had her reservations about letting Lascarina sail, but she herself had insisted that all her children—girls and boys—learn to read, write and use numbers.

"Why are you doing that? It's a waste of time!" argued the village women, who knew full well that a woman's lot in life was to marry young and have many children.

Some of the men were even more ominous: "You will make your daughter a spinster," they muttered. "No man in his right mind would marry a girl who knows how to read. Educated women are disobedient, nothing but trouble!"

Captain Lazarou roared with laughter when he heard this. "Well, Paraskevi," he said cheerfully, "now we know why you are so troublesome! How dare you think for yourself!"

The criticism, however, stung Paraskevi, for she hardly wanted to provide the villagers with more reason for gossip. "You never know what life has in store for you," she answered them pleasantly. "Where would I have been when I found my-self alone here on Spetses, had I not known my letters and numbers?" This answer only reminded the islanders of her mysterious arrival on Spetses and prompted more questions. "Sometimes you just can't win," thought Paraskevi to herself, and resolved to ignore their remarks.

There were no organized schools on the Greek islands or on the mainland. The Ottoman overlords did not expressly forbid their subjects from learning their own language, but their *beys* could choose to make life very difficult for instructors. Often it was the local priest, rarely well-educated himself, who taught. He risked his safety and sometimes his life so that the children of his village could learn at least enough to read the Bible and understand their history. On Spetses, Father Spiros set up a makeshift classroom in the cellar of his church. He encouraged parents to send their daughters to school, but few did. Though he was glad to have had a chance to guide Lascarina's beliefs, by this time Father Spiros realized that there was little more he could teach her. It was from Lazarou's small collection of books by English and French philosophers that Lascarina now read, learning about the ideas of freedom and equality that were sweeping across Europe.

Paraskevi and Lazarou decided that Lascarina's view of the world should include more than the neighboring Saronic islands. Even in Spetses, it was clear that the Ottoman Empire was under attack from all sides: Russians from the North, Bedouins from the South, and the Sultan's own rebellious Albanian *pashas* in the West. The desperate Sultan tried to defend his domain by taxing his subjects more and more heavily to raise money for his armies and by conscripting Greek men into his navy.

"We don't know when the next revolt will break out," said Lazarou. "It's best that our children learn as much as they can about their own people." Paraskevi nodded, remembering the disastrous years before Lascarina's birth when the disorganized Greeks failed to see that they had to pull together.

Lascarina started traveling with Lazarou, keeping his books and writing up contracts with the merchants whose goods he carried. Sometimes her oldest half-brother, Nicholas, joined them; she was grateful for his company, for he was good-humored and thoughtful and a keen sailor too. They journeyed just beyond Hydra, to Athens, then a quiet port town on the mainland. The sparkling white marble Parthenon was perched on the acropolis, high above the sleepy village.

Lascarina gasped. "Look, Nicholas! There it is—Pericles's splendid temple!"

"I just read about it with Father Spiros," said Nicholas. "Pericles built it right after all the Greeks came together to drive back the Persians."

Further down the coast, they came to bustling Gytheio, the main port of the southern Greek peninsula, the Peloponnesus. All the talk there was of the capture by pirates of a ship that had left Gytheio a month before. Now that the Ottomans were less able to police the seas, raiders from North Africa's Barbary Coast no longer felt the need to cooperate with or obey the Turks. Crews of lightly armed merchant ships—sailing under any flag—were targets to be robbed and sold into slavery, or murdered.

"We just heard that all of the crew were brought to the slave market in Algiers," a townsman told Lazarou, "except for five Maniati who died fighting."

"I'm not surprised that they fought to the death," said Lazarou, "but what on earth were men from the Mani doing at sea?"

"Mavromichaelis was sending them to parley with Kolokotronis, on Corfu."

"Kolokotronis on Corfu?" Lazarou was puzzled that the Peloponnesus's famous warrior and political leader should be on an island then owned by Venice.

"Yes," said the townsman, "hiding from the Ottomans."

"And probably also trying to buy weapons from the

Venetians," mused Lazarou. "It sounds to me as if rebellion is brewing—and what better place for it to start than the Mani."

"I doubt it," said the townsman. "It would be strange indeed for revolution to break out in the one part of Greece where the Turks never set foot!" A look of resentment crossed his face. "Besides," he continued, "those mountaineers haven't suffered nearly as much as we have here on the coast. I'm about to lose my store, thanks to the new tax on sales. The Ottomans will make us all beggars."

"Who *are* these Maniati?" asked Lascarina. "Where do they come from?"

"You see those mountains over there?" Lascarina looked where the townsman pointed. The rugged Taygetos mountains loomed dark on the horizon. "Just behind them is Mani."

"A rock-strewn, lawless land," said Lazarou, "where blood feuds still flourish."

The townsman snorted. "Yes. It's no surprise the Turks never wanted it."

"Oh, but they did," said Lazarou thoughtfully. "The mountain gorges ran red with blood every time they tried to invade. And mark my words: Mani *will* be the cradle of our freedom. Mavromichaelis and Kolokotronis, Black Michael and the Old Man of the Mountains: they are beginning to lay the groundwork for a revolution."

Just at that moment, there was a great racket. A band of six men on horseback galloped into Gytheio, their swords and muskets clanging against heavy shields.

"Perfect timing!" cried the townsman, turning to Lascarina. "These, my dear, are our famous warriors, our *armatoloi*."

Lascarina stared at the men. All wore coarse white woolen kilts, *fustanellas*, and ragged cotton shirts and vests. Two were barefoot. "I didn't think anyone dressed like that anymore,"

she said. "They look like the ancient Greeks who fought in the
Trojan War, as if they've stepped straight out of *The Iliad*. And
why do some wear no boots?"

The townsman chuckled. "It's a mark of honor among the
Maniati. They boast that all their money goes for weapons."

Lazarou's next trip took them through the choppy seas
around the tip of Mani, north to Igoumenitsa, the main port

of western Greece. "Here," he said to Lascarina and Nicholas, "you will stay on board the ship. You may take short strolls in the port, but always with one of my crew, and you will then return to quarters. You must never leave the port." His voice was unusually stern. Clearly the captain intended to proceed on his own to the mountain town of Ioannina, the heart of Epirus, where he would meet with some merchants—furriers—to arrange the transport of fox and bear pelts.

"But why?" protested Nicholas. "I had been wanting to see the fortress of Ali Pasha." Lascarina was disappointed too.

"And risk being stolen—right off the street—to become the Pasha's slaves?" Lascarina and Nicholas were stunned to hear the Captain raise his voice. "Ali Pasha is ruthless to the Greeks. He's an Albanian Muslim, a vassal of the Sultan, but it's an open secret that he's plotting against him. He is treacherous as a viper. Even the Turks despise him." Lazarou paused and said more calmly, "On the other hand, I wish you *could* meet the merchants I'm going to see. Many are Romaniote, Jewish people who have lived up there for centuries, keeping the faith we read about in the Old Testament. Fascinating."

Though they would not admit it, Lascarina and Nicholas felt their own hearts sink when Lazarou mounted a mule for the trek up the steep trails to Ioannina. His pistol was strapped to his chest, under his cape, and across the saddle of his guide's mule was an old musket, loaded. "Please be careful," whispered Lascarina.

In the streets of Igoumenitsa, the people talked of ten Greek sailors who had recently been impressed into the Sultan's navy. "It is only a matter of time before they begin the *paidom-azoma* again," they muttered. They remembered the tales their grandparents told of the grim day that fell once each decade, when Ottoman army officers would sweep through the villages of their conquered peoples to take away all boys aged five years. These children were raised as Turks and joined the Sultan's most elite military corps, the Janissaries. By the time they were sent into battle, they had forgotten their roots: they would fight ferociously for the only family they knew, the Ottoman army. The dialect spoken by the people of Epirus contained many Turkish words and was sometimes incomprehensible to Lascarina—but she could feel their terror.

She and Nicholas were relieved to see Lazarou return. He rode at the head of a train of mules, each laden with two large wooden crates on either side. Lascarina quickly drafted a contract to be delivered to the Romaniote merchants for the transport and sale of their furs. "The people here," she said to Lazarou, "are so different from those we met in Gytheio. You spoke of rebellion brewing in Mani. Do you really think that the people of Epirus and the Peloponnesus will unite against the Turks?"

"We must be sure of it," said Lazarou grimly. "Otherwise, our next struggle for freedom is doomed again to fail."

When she returned to Spetses after this trip, she visited Soula, eager to tell her of the places she had seen. But Soula had news of her own: "Petros and I are engaged," she called as soon as she saw Lascarina. Soula beamed with happiness, and Lascarina felt her own heart leap with joy for her friend. At the same time, though, her throat tightened. She had confided everything to Soula. Who would she speak with now?

As if she'd read Lascarina's mind, Soula said, "We will still be friends. And soon enough, you'll be married too. We will have plenty to talk about."

Lascarina burst into laughter. "Soula, you are dreaming. Who would even think of me as anything but a helper to my mother and the Captain?"

"You've been the talk of the town ever since that race," protested Soula.

"Yes, but that doesn't mean any of the young men would want to *marry* me," said Lascarina. "They already have me pegged for a spinster." She paused and mused, "And maybe that is not the worst fate in the world."

"What about Captain Bouboulis? I was standing right next to you when he congratulated you—*I* saw how he looked at you."

Lascarina could not help but blush. "He will be lucky to come home alive. And it has been two years since the race—he will surely have met so many women, women who are more beautiful, more wealthy, who have seen so much more of the world than I have." She grew thoughtful. "Soula, how do you know that Petros is the right man for you?"

"Well," said Soula slowly, considering this question carefully, "there is nothing hidden between us. Petros likes me just the way I am. And in my case, there is no question that he is marrying me for a dowry."

Lascarina hugged her friend. "Let me know if you need any help with cooking or baking for the feast! And you know that I for sure hope to dance at your wedding."

"Yes!" said Soula cheerfully, for she knew her friend loved to dance. "We *will* have music! My mother found an old Roma woman at the market—she said there are musicians now in their camp, and they will play for us."

The Roma people were called "gypsies" by most Greeks. No one knew where they originally came from—perhaps India, some conjectured—but now they wandered through much of Central Europe and even occasionally reached the islands, setting up camps of huts or tents or, in Spetses, settling in caves on the rugged north coast. They rarely stayed anywhere for more than a few years. They did not mix much with the people of the regions through which they traveled, for they were viewed by the natives with suspicion and blamed for any crime in the communities near their camps. Only as musicians were they welcome, for all knew that the Roma spoke more eloquently than any other people through their music—of grief, violence, and loneliness, but also of joy, love, and freedom.

The very evening after Lascarina's conversation with Soula, a winter storm blew into Spetses, driving a cold, hard rain over the island. Shortly after night had fallen and the younger children had gone to bed, Lascarina, Paraskevi, and Lazarou heard a knock at the front door.

"Who could it be, in this weather?" asked Paraskevi.

Lazarou carried a candle to the door. "Who's there?" he asked.

The voice that answered was husky and low, yet strangely musical: "Beka, Beka of the Romani."

Lazarou opened the door and saw a girl who appeared to be about Lascarina's age. She was drenched and shivering. Her flimsy, ragged cape looked as if it had been worn for weeks. Wisps of black hair hung from beneath her soaked headscarf. Still, her dark brown eyes gazed solemnly and steadily, without fear, at the three people gathered inside the door. She clutched at some bundle under her cape.

"I returned to Spetses yesterday and am trying to reach my people in the caves. I must have taken a wrong turn on the road from the dock. May I stay in your barn until this storm passes?"

Paraskevi looked at her with concern. "What is that which you hold under your cape? A child?"

Beka shook her head and pulled out a wooden case. "It is my father's violin. He went to Salonika to visit his best friend…," a note of bitterness crept into her voice as she added, "…who had been accused of a robbery and put in jail. I traveled with him, as he had been unwell for some time. There, in Salonika, he died." Tears filled her eyes as she said, "We had to bury him there."

"We are sorry for you," said Paraskevi. "Come in. Sit and eat something."

As Paraskevi prepared a plate for Beka, Lascarina took her to the pump in the courtyard. Beka washed the grime from her travel off her hands and face, and they returned to the table, where Paraskevi had set a plate piled with thick slabs of bread, feta cheese, and olives. Beka ate ravenously, for she had not had food in two days. A steaming cup of tea appeared on the table as well; Beka sipped it and felt the chill that had settled inside her evaporate.

After Beka had eaten her fill, Lascarina said, "Just this afternoon, my friend told me that a troupe of Roma musicians are on the island. They will play at her wedding."

"Yes," nodded Beka. "Those musicians are my family. I will play with them," she said, lifting her chin proudly. "That is why I am so grateful to sleep in your barn, to get my father's violin out of the rain."

"No need for you to sleep in the barn," said Lazarou with a smile. "We have a spare room."

Beka looked incredulous. "You are willing to let *me*, a Roma, sleep in your house?"

"Are you suggesting we count our silver pieces now?" said Lazarou drily.

For a moment, Beka's face darkened, and Lazarou regretted his sarcastic joke. "Excuse me," he said, "I was mocking my people, not yours." Then Beka smiled, a weary smile for a girl so young.

"Thank you," she said. "You know that we are not used to being treated kindly. I have nothing to give you, but I will play for you some music."

She unlocked the wooden case using a key that she kept on a ribbon around her neck. Gently, tenderly, as if it were indeed a child, she lifted out a violin, polished so that shades of red shone through its brown veneer. She tightened the horse hair on her bow, turned the violin's tuning pegs, and played a haunting Roma air that spoke of grief and longing and hope all at once. Then she pointed the bow at Lascarina and said, "Miss, someday soon I will play at your wedding." Lascarina blushed and shook her head. "Yes," said Beka firmly and launched into a series of Greek dances, some graceful, some wild, all joyful.

The family sat in silence for a moment after Beka had finished. "In all my days," said Paraskevi finally, "I have never heard such playing. Your father must have been a master, and you his pride and joy."

Again Beka's eyes filled with tears. She locked the violin in its case. "I will leave very early tomorrow. I know my granny is worried about me." Lazarou carefully explained which path she needed to follow to get to the caves, and Paraskevi led her into the guest room, where Beka collapsed into an exhausted slumber.

At dawn, Lascarina heard her padding down the stairs. "Wait a moment," she called, running to pack some bread and hard cheese. "For your travels," she said, wrapping the food in a towel and handing it to Beka.

"Thank you," said the girl, with the same serious expression she wore the night before. "I will see you again." Without another word, she turned and made her way along the path Lazarou had described.

Later that day, Paraskevi sent Lascarina to the village smith with a copper pot that needed repair. Lascarina saw that a two-masted ship, rigged fore-and-aft, had dropped anchor in the harbor.

"I've never seen such a vessel," she said to the smith, handing him the pot and standing close to his hearth to warm herself. The days were becoming chilly.

"Why, that's a schooner," said the smith, pausing his manipulation of the pot in the blaze, pleased for once to be privy to interesting news before someone else in the village. "Haven't you heard? Captain Bouboulis is back. He had a skirmish with pirates...."

"Oh! Is the Captain safe?"

"I said he was back, didn't I? Now, let me finish. He managed to score a direct hit on the corsair and escaped. His own barque was damaged, but all his cargo was intact. So he made it to Le Havre. His profits were so great that he had this new ship built while the *Elpida* was repaired—she will be good as new. And now he's back in Spetses to rest for a while."

Lascarina raced home, clutching the slightly lopsided pot.

"Was someone chasing you?" asked Paraskevi as she examined the pot.

"The smith just told me that Captain Bouboulis is back! He'll be staying here for some time now."

"Hmm...Did he marry?"

Lascarina forgot how, just the day before, she herself had told Soula that Dimitri would have met many potential brides over the past two years. She stared at her mother mutely.

A Secret Revealed

Dimitri did not lack for company on Spetses. Every afternoon, as he strolled from his ship to the inn, a crowd of sailors and captains, mostly Spetsiotes, gathered around him. They would lead him to the taverna and bombard him with questions.

"Tell us, what manner of craft are the Barbary pirates sailing these days?"

"How many Ottoman frigates did you see? Did they stop you?"

"How are the waters beyond the Straits?"

"How does your schooner sail?"

Late one evening, Dimitri casually asked a question of his own: "And what about Spetses's lady sailor? Has she won any more races?"

The men laughed. One said, "You mean Lascarina, Captain Lazarou's stepdaughter? That one will be sailing alone for the rest of her life. Who could live with such a headstrong woman?"

"I hear," said another, "that Lazarou takes her along on many of his trips. She keeps his books for him and then comes back to help her mother with that passel of children up in their house. All the makings of an old maid, I think."

"Never mind that," said a third. "My parents told me that no one here knows who her father is. There seems to be some scandal surrounding Paraskevi."

Dimitri scowled. How could these men, all decent enough, believe such stories? His parents had always spoken highly of Lazarou. Surely any woman he married would be worthy of respect. And as for the headstrong Lascarina—he decided to see her again for himself.

Dimitri started attending church. The whitewashed chapel was perched in a clearing at the top of a hill—the same hill on which the Lazarou house was built, but further up. It was three hundred years old and had escaped pirate raids and the devastation of 1771 only because it was far inland. Like most Greek Orthodox churches, even this small one had a dome and a belfry from which bells summoned islanders to church each Sunday.

He positioned himself in a corner of the church that offered a clear view of the women's section. The first time she caught a glimpse of him, Lascarina smiled—and then blushed. Dimitri raised his eyebrows in mock surprise—but, to his chagrin, felt his own face reddening as well. She was the same direct, bright-eyed young woman he remembered—clearly not "headstrong," as she listened carefully to the priest and spoke with courtesy and good humor to family and neighbors. On her part, Lascarina noted with relief that there was no evidence of a wife: the curly-haired captain always arrived at and left the church alone.

Dimitri resolved to speak with Lazarou at the first opportunity. This did not present itself until the older captain returned from a voyage to the mainland. Dimitri hovered around the dock, waiting for Lazarou to pay his crew and settle his accounts with the island merchants. Finally, just as the sun set, Lazarou turned to walk home. Dimitri sprinted over to him.

"Dimitri!" cried Lazarou, beaming. "What a wonderful surprise! Word of your adventure with the Barbary pirates reached me even in the North."

As they shook hands, Lazarou noticed that the young man's palms were moist and his face, anxious.

"Captain Lazarou, I'm sorry to delay you. I know that you are tired and eager to go home. But I would like to ask you something regarding your stepdaughter."

"Lascarina? Well, go ahead."

Dimitri's words tumbled out in a rush. "If Lascarina were like other women, I would at this moment be asking you for her hand. Believe me, I have had several opportunities to marry over the past couple of years."

"Yes," said Lazarou with a grin. "I seem to remember hearing something about this from Captain Stenohori. In fact, he gave me a hat to return to you."

"Oh…Well…That was just one of many introductions. But Lascarina is different from these others, and I have come to think, well, umm, that…that I would like to marry her. She needs to decide for herself though. Will you let her do that? Will you let her talk with me?"

In the dusk, Dimitri could not discern the twinkle in Lazarou's eyes. "So, you are asking me if you may—what is that new-fangled word—*court* her?'

"Uh, yes."

"That English custom could further damage the reputation of my family. I am sure you've heard that there is some question about the identity of Lascarina's father."

"Well, yes…"

Lazarou peered closely at Dimitri. "You are rising rapidly in the world, even among the Russians and Ukrainians in Odessa. The possibility of something 'not right' about our background does not bother you?"

"No."

"And you know, Paraskevi and I have had four children together. We will not be able to give Lascarina much of a dowry."

Even in the evening shadows, Lazarou could see the color rise in the young man's face.

"How could you say such a thing?" said Dimitri hotly. "The incident with Stenohori should have shown you that I am *not* for sale to the family that offers the highest bid! I am a successful captain, like yourself, well able to support a wife and children."

Lazarou chuckled. "Relax, my friend. I did not mean to offend you. I agree with your plan. However," he said, a note of worry creeping into his voice, "I do need to discuss this with Paraskevi. If I can persuade her, I will send word to you to come by our house this Sunday afternoon."

Paraskevi was not pleased with the concept of 'courting.'

"Lazarou, haven't we generated enough gossip? You yourself said Lascarina was smitten with Dimitri. Yes, I know that was more than two years ago—but I can see that she still is. Let's just arrange this and be done with it. Lascarina will be happy."

"She may be happy, but she will only be confident if the decision is in her hands. Paraskevi, you know your daughter."

Paraskevi had to admit that Lazarou was right, but that did not stop her from grumbling the rest of the week—to Lascarina's complete bewilderment—about the English and their ridiculous notions of romance.

Dimitri raced to the Lazarou house early Sunday afternoon before any other visitors had arrived. He spied Lascarina in the garden. "Would you like to see my new schooner?" he called. "I am on my way to the dock now. I remember what a good sailor you are."

Lascarina stood speechless for an instant. Then, without any hesitation, as if in a dream, she removed her apron, brushed back her hair, and said, "I would like that very much." She stepped into the house and called to her parents, "I'm going with Captain Bouboulis to see his new ship, okay? I'll be home soon." Back outside, she fell into step with Dimitri.

Lascarina's comment did not immediately register with Paraskevi. Only when she caught sight of the two turning a bend in the path did she realize what Lascarina had said. She rushed toward the door.

"Paraskevi, stop! Where are you going?" cried Captain Lazarou.

"Lascarina and Dimitri are walking down the path *together*. You said he would speak with her here! We need to join them, or the whole village will be talking."

Lazarou knew well that an unmarried girl walking with a man and no chaperone would be slandered. But at this hour, no one was likely to be out and about. Sunday visits would not begin until later in the day. "Please, Paraskevi, calm down. Everything will be fine."

Paraskevi glared at him but remained in the house.

Meanwhile, Dimitri was starting to guide Lascarina about the vessel. "You see that, on a schooner, all of the lower masts have fore-and-aft sails. This makes the ship easier to maneuver than a barque or brig, and crews can be smaller."

And so he continued…for two hours. Lascarina soon had an encyclopedic knowledge of schooners—their construction, history, and speed in all weather conditions. The wintry afternoon sunlight was fading. She knew that she could stay no longer and felt an ache in her heart.

With all the boldness of one who feels a dream slipping away, she looked squarely into Dimitri's eyes. "Thank you for showing me about," she said. "A captain like you deserves such a fine ship. Darkness is falling, though, and I must be on my way, alone. Is there nothing else I should know?"

Dimitri realized that his opportunity was about to vanish. He took Lascarina's hand. "Forgive me for rambling like this. I am beginning to see that I am something of a coward when it comes to affairs of the heart. I did not bring you here for a lecture, but rather to umm, to…to propose that we spend the rest of our lives together. Will you, uh, marry me?"

Tears of happiness welled up in Lascrina's eyes. "I was afraid you would never ask! You are sure that you like me as I am?"

Dimitri laughed. "Just the way you are, Lascarina, you brighten my life. Now, what say you?"

"Yes," whispered Lascarina. "Yes," she said again, as Dimitri's lips brushed softly against hers.

It was with much relief that Lazarou spotted the couple returning, hand in hand. Some of the neighbors who had stopped in to visit had asked where Lascarina was, and Paraskevi, tight-lipped, had left him to invent excuses for her absence. Fortunately, the last guest had departed some time ago.

A smile spread across Paraskevi's face as Lascarina announced her plans to marry Dimitri "right after Christmas."

"Just a moment," said Paraskevi, her laughter ringing through the room as if from a bell that Lascarina had never heard before. "We are going to have a proper wedding, and, Dimitri, whether you want one or not, you *will* have a dowry, at least of linens and household furnishings. We have much to prepare."

She fell silent for a few moments, and when she spoke next, her voice was strained. "Lascarina, you know that I promised to one day tell you who your father was. Now is the time for Lazarou and me to do that, now when we are sure you will be able to keep the secret we have guarded for so many years—if not for your own safety, then for that of Dimitri and, someday, your children." She turned to Lazarou. "Please, could you sail to Hydra tomorrow and bring Ioannis here? I want my brother to be with us when we tell Lascarina and Dimitri, for, without him, I could never have come home to these islands."

The next evening, Lazarou returned with Uncle Ioannis, who shook Dimitri's hand heartily and welcomed him to the family. The younger children had been sent to Soula, and the rest of the family gathered around the indoor hearth, away from the chilly evening air—and from any neighbors who might come upon them.

"Lascarina," started Paraskevi, "you were born in Constantinople on May 11, 1771. Ioannis and I had sailed there to visit your father, who was imprisoned in the Sultan's dungeon."

"Imprisoned," whispered Lascarina, horrified.

"Yes. Stavrianos Pinotsis…"

"Stavrianos Pinotsis!" exclaimed Dimitri. "I have heard of him! The only one of the captains from Hydra who took part in the Orloff Rebellion!"

"Yes," said Ioannis, "and for that the Turks hunted him down in Odessa. He had gone up there to accept a new commission, directly from Secretary Orloff, as commander of the Greek Aegean fleet. The place was swarming with spies, and he was betrayed. And the Russians, who had encouraged our revolt, who had promised support, turned their backs on us as soon as they secured access to the Bosphorus Strait through a treaty with the Ottomans."

"Yes," said Paraskevi bitterly, "I had begged Stavrianos *not* to fight. My parents and I, we told him Greece was unprepared. Even *he* was worried that we Greeks had not really planned that revolt. No one believed that the Russians aimed purely to free us—fellow Orthodox Christians—from the Ottoman yoke. But Stavrianos thought it was a matter of honor—and he had devised an Aegean strategy that he was sure would undo the Turks."

"And it probably would have," said Ioannis. "The Hydriote captains held back until they could see whether other European powers would support this strategy—but after Stavrianos was arrested, those plans fell apart."

"Here on Spetses, though," said Paraskevi, "a few courageous—or maybe rash—captains did take up arms." She smiled and gestured to Lazarou, who remained silent, lost in his own memories of that time.

"How on earth did you get to Constantinople to see Stavrianos?" asked Dimitri.

"We traveled to Corfu and paid a Venetian captain from there to carry us to Constantinople," said Ioannis. "Of course, we took the greatest care to keep the Ottoman soldiers who had been stationed on Hydra from learning that Paraskevi was Stavrianos's wife; they would have jailed our entire family had they found out. It was a stormy voyage, rough for Paraskevi, who was heavily pregnant. And we were stunned by the immensity and tumult of Constantinople—we had never seen so many people of so many different races: Slavs, Greeks, Turks, Jews, Arabs, Asians, Africans. We were almost torn apart by the crush of the crowd."

"Someday, soon, you too will see Constantinople," said Dimitri to Lascarina. She nodded.

"Ioannis, remember how that Greek trader, Chrysophilos, came to our rescue?" mused Paraskevi. "We must have looked thoroughly lost. He volunteered to help us but became quite nervous when we told him we needed to find the prison—and when we revealed why Stavrianos had been jailed, he almost abandoned us. He was terrified that the Turks might perceive him as the friend of a rebel. He explained how the Sultan retaliated against all Greeks in the city whenever there was even a whiff of rebellion from the Greek provinces. Chrysophilos just wanted to live in peace with his family—he was content to coexist with the Turks, on their terms."

"Well, at least he stuck with us," said Ioannis. "He took us to the prison. The guard agreed to lead me down to the dungeon where Stavrianos lay, warning me to take this as a lesson. He was astonished when Paraskevi insisted on accompanying us, but he let her. We climbed down a steep, spiral stairwell. At the bottom, we stood in pitch darkness, supporting ourselves against the slimy stone walls. Another guard appeared with a torch and motioned for us to follow. Rats scurried out of our path as we made our way through the cells. In the shadows, the prisoners sat huddled in rags—debtors, thieves, murderers, and revolutionaries—here, they all looked alike."

"Mama," whispered Lascarina, "you were so brave. What happened?"

"We found your father lying on a wooden pallet, his body little more than a skeleton covered with skin. I could not believe this was the handsome captain I had married just two years before. The guard roused him with a kick and said, 'We are supposed to hang him tomorrow, but he might save us the trouble.'"

Lascarina gasped.

"Stavrianos turned to me," continued Paraskevi. "At first, he thought he was dreaming. 'It is a miracle you are here,' he finally whispered. I was amazed that he had the strength to take my hand. He told us how he had been arrested and asked for news of the Rebellion. We had to tell him it was crushed, that none of the other Hydriote captains had joined, that hundreds of Ottoman troops had been stationed on Hydra, and that regiments from Albania were burning Spetses—Stavrianos moaned when he heard this. Still, he said, with a force that surprised me, 'Promise that you will keep the flame of freedom burning in our child.' I promised—and said also that I would find a priest to give him the last rites. We embraced one final time, and the guard let us out."

Ioannis took up the story. "I was astonished to see Chrysophilos still waiting for us. When we told him we needed a priest, he took us to the Greek quarter, where we found a Father Constantinou. He had often ministered to Greek prisoners in the dungeon, and he rushed there with his chalice to find Stavrianos. Paraskevi's labor started as soon as she entered the priest's home. His sister, who kept house for him, ran out to find a midwife." Ioannis turned to Lascarina. "When the midwife saw your mother and heard her story, she told me that she did not think you would survive. So we were all overjoyed to hear the priest's house echo with your cries. You were tiny but strong. We named you Lascarina, after Stavrianos's mother.

Stavrianos died shortly after receiving the Sacrament, before the Turks could hang him. Within three days, we buried him in the old Christian cemetery and christened you."

"Yes, we were exhausted," said Paraskevi. "We paid another Venetian captain to bring us back to Hydra, though Ioannis had warned from the beginning that I should go to Spetses instead. He argued that Hydra would be swarming with Ottoman troops and that they would soon discover who I was. On the other hand, the Albanian regiments had been withdrawn from Spetses; after they had pillaged the island, there was really no reason for them to stay. Only one Ottoman official remained there—the tax collector, Mustafa. I was terrified at the thought of living alone on Spetses, but it wasn't until I saw twenty Ottoman warships anchored in Hydra's harbor that I knew Ioannis was right. We asked the Venetian to sail on to Spetses—and paid him handsomely from our dwindling supply of gold ducats. Ioannis knew that our family had for centuries owned some land on Spetses and had the foresight to carry the deed to this land with him. We showed it to Mustafa. As did the few remaining Spetsiotes, Mustafa thought that I was an unwed mother being sent away by her Hydriote family into hiding. Ioannis toiled for weeks to make the ramshackle cottage we found on the property fit for us to live in. He restored the old well to working order and cleared a small space for me to farm. And then, he could stay no longer—our parents needed help, and my sister's husband needed a captain for the ship he had just built. Ioannis returned to Spetses as often as he could—without arousing suspicions."

Finally Lazarou spoke. "After the Rebellion collapsed, Captain Solaris and I hid for two years, here on Spetses, in the caves to the North. The Turks burned our ships and murdered Captain Solaris's wife and children. For some months, I feared he would lose his mind. Somehow, Father Spiros found us and brought us food and news from the village, which was slowly rising from its ashes. At last it was safe to return. Little by little, we found work as captains and rebuilt our lives. And then, on one of my trips to Hydra, I met Ioannis. In short order, he introduced me to Paraskevi."

Paraskevi resumed the story: "Never had I thought I would have another chance at happiness." She smiled at Lazarou and continued. "Now, Lascarina, you can understand why we kept the identity of your father a secret—and why you must continue to do so."

Dimitri murmured, almost to himself, "I can see I am marrying into a family of extraordinary women."

Lazarou said to Ioannis, "We've set the wedding date for the sixth of June. If it is safe, perhaps you can bring your parents?"

"I pray it may be so," answered Ioannis. "They are overjoyed with their granddaughter's choice, and are already planning a story for the *Bey*."

Lascarina smiled and hugged him.

Within weeks, Dimitri hired architects, stonemasons, and carpenters to build a fine new home near the harbor. "The time has come for us to take back our shores," he announced to those who wondered why he did not seek the safety of the island's interior. A graceful palazzo arose by the sea, well suited to the rocky site, its loggia stating quite clearly that the architect had looked west, not east, for inspiration. Included in the cargo carried during Dimitri's next few voyages was furniture made in France and Russia for the large rooms of the new house.

Lascarina's heart fluttered with both pride and apprehension: "How am I to manage this palazzo?" she asked Paraskevi and Lazarou.

They laughed, for rarely had they seen Lascarina so flustered. "Don't worry," said Paraskevi. "You will have servants—I will teach you to supervise them, and before you know it, you will turn the palazzo into a home. Dimitri will be proud of you."

Next, Dimitri turned his attention to his new schooner. He had it scrubbed and polished from stem to stern. Finally, he named it: the *Capitanissa*—the Captain's Wife. Lascarina realized that the time had come for her to give up the *Dolphin*. "Were it not for this dear, trim sloop," she thought, "I would never have met Dimitri." She entrusted the sailboat to Nicholas.

The Lazarou household buzzed with excitement. All the splendid embroidery on Lascarina's wedding clothes had to be completed, and on the linens and bed coverings in her dowry as well. Two weeks before the wedding, it was time to roll out the leaves of pastry—phyllo—needed for the pies and desserts that would be served at the wedding feast. Soula rounded up the women in her family and brought them with her to help.

The villagers shook their heads in amazement, still wondering how their gallant Captain Bouboulis could have chosen this strange young woman as his bride. But this did not keep them from crowding into Spetses's small chapel on the wedding day.

That morning, Lascarina rose early and walked quietly through the home where she had grown up, remembering how she had seen much of it being built. She gazed out to sea from the veranda, trying to calm her fluttering heart. She donned the traditional wedding attire of the Saronic islands: a long crimson velvet vest heavily embroidered with gold, over a silk dress with a full skirt and long lace cuffs. On her head was a lace scarf from Venice; about her neck, many strands of gold coins; and at her waist, a magnificent gold buckle studded with pearls.

Lascarina walked, surrounded by her family, up the steep hillside path to the chapel. The service started. Smoke from burning incense swirled around the gilded icons of saints and prophets which were mounted on a screen before the altar. Hymns were sung and prayers recited. Finally, the priest placed wedding crowns of gold on the heads of the bride and groom, symbolizing the glory and honor that were theirs, and exchanged the crowns three times. From this point forward, Lascarina was called Bouboulina, as it was the custom for a wife to take on a feminine form of her husband's last name.

The guests poured out of the church and made their way to the bride's home, where they sat down to a splendid feast: red wine from the island's vineyards, roast lamb, olives, *tiropites*—puffed pastries stuffed with cheese—and baklava made of ground nuts and phyllo and smothered in syrup.

Just as they were starting dessert, strains of lively dance tunes floated into the courtyard. A troupe of Roma musicians, headed by none other than Beka, had wended their way down from the northern hills to the wedding party, playing their instruments as they passed through the stone arch. Beka was no longer wrapped in a ragged cape. She wore a flounced black skirt embroidered with red and turquoise flowers and a brilliant red blouse. Her glistening black hair was pulled back, and her dark eyes sparkled. As soon as she saw Lascarina, she again pointed her

bow at her and said in her low, husky voice, "You see, I was right! May you have much happiness with your handsome captain!"

The guests danced to the lively tunes of fiddles and clarinets. Paraskevi and Lazarou were the first to lead the circle of dancers, then Dimitri, leaping with joy, and Lascarina, beaming, her steps in perfect time with the intricate rhythms. *Everyone*—even grandfathers and grandmothers—joined the dance, for it was their way of honoring the new couple and sharing in their happiness. The band played until daybreak, but at midnight, the bride and groom bid Paraskevi and Lazarou and all the guests farewell, boarded the *Capitanissa* and embarked on their first voyage together.

V

The Capitanissa

For their wedding trip, Dimitri and Lascarina sailed to Odessa on the northwest coast of the Black Sea. It had long been a cosmopolitan city, built on trade: thousands of Greeks, Central Europeans, Ukrainians and Russians—Christians and Jews—lived together with Muslim Ottoman Turks. And it remained a hotbed of intrigue. In 1790, the city was still part of the Ottoman empire, but soon it would be won by Russia, and the Russian Empress, Catherine, would issue a decree for the construction of splendid new palaces. From early on, the Russians and Greeks conspired against the Turks; they shared a common religion, but in truth, the Russian leaders did not hesitate to use the Greeks as pawns to expand their territory, while the Greeks squeezed whatever financial support they could from the Russians, to support their struggle for independence from the Ottomans.

Lascarina saw Dimitri's fleet—three brigs, two barques, including the restored *Elpida*, and two other schooners—docked in Odessa. "But why keep them here instead of Spetses?" she asked him.

"It will not be long before Odessa is in Russian hands," said Dimitri. "When that happens, they will be safer here."

As they were returning to Spetses, Dimitri sighed. "I have spent months at sea and never felt lonely. Now, it will be different—I will miss you when I am away."

"Well, that problem is easily solved," said Lascarina. "I will sail with you."

Dimitri gazed at her. "I was hoping you might want to do that. But are you sure? The Black Sea and the eastern Mediterranean can be rough."

"Of course I am sure," said Lascarina. "I am not prone to seasickness. And besides, Captain Bouboulis, I've noticed that you need some help with your bookkeeping."

Dimitri grinned. "Hmm. Very observant of you. It's true enough that I've ended up on the short end in a few of my business deals."

The ship's crew, who had been warned by the Captain to behave like gentlemen when his new bride was on board, had looked forward to depositing her back in Spetses at the end of this voyage and resuming their sailor-like ways. It was with dismay, then, that they heard Dimitri say, when they reached Spetses, "We will stay here for two weeks to allow the Capitanissa to repack her trunks, and then we sail for Salonika."

"But Captain!" cried the first mate, Harry. "Who will tend to your fine new home? The Capitanissa surely would rather set up house than roam the seas with us."

Dimitri let the Capitanissa speak for herself. "All in good time, Harry," she said gently. "I will be of greater help to my husband if I learn something about his work. And I count on you, next to the Captain, to help me."

With this compliment, Harry beamed and held his head high. The other sailors shifted uneasily. Dimitri worried that he was about to lose his crew. "Don't look so down-hearted, men," he said. "You will not see the Capitanissa on deck too often. She will be in my study most of the time, working on our accounts."

"You mean," shouted one of the sailors, "that *she* is to be our *paymaster*?"

"Um, yes," said the Captain.

After Dimitri and Lascarina debarked, the sailors gathered around Harry. "What are we going to do?" they grumbled. "We'll be the laughingstock of every port once it's learned we're being paid by a *woman*."

Harry tugged at his ample mustache as he thought for a moment. "Men," he said finally, "I have been with Dimitri for as long as he's been a captain. A more courageous man you will not find. I don't intend to leave him now, even if maybe he has gone a little crazy. Anyone who can't bring himself to collect his pay with good grace from a lady, don't bother signing up for our next voyage." Loyalty to Dimitri and Harry outweighed the sailors' fear of ridicule. They all remained with the *Capitanissa*, although not one breathed a word to crews from other ships about the strange business practices of their captain.

Over the next three years, Lascarina spent more time at sea than in her new palazzo. When she was not balancing ledgers and counting out gold ducats, she strolled on deck, learning all she could about how the three kinds of ships in Dimitri's fleet were rigged and sailed. Lascarina and Dimitri took their first two children—sons Yiannis and Georgios—on almost every voyage. A cradle was installed in the captain's quarters, and a nanny hired to watch the boys every second of the day to keep them out of the crew's way—and stop them from falling overboard.

On a voyage to Igoumenitsa—the Epirote port controlled by the vicious Ali Pasha, where Lazarou had warned his children never to go exploring—Lascarina saw a sight that would haunt her all her life. A gallows had been erected near the harbor, and dangling from it was a man. As they pulled into the harbor, they saw that the man was a priest. In front of the gallows was a sign reading, "Thus be it to all teachers of sedition." From the terrified Greeks in the port they learned that, in a fit of rage, Ali Pasha had seized the priest and charged him with treason—only because he was teaching the children of his village to read. "There will be no more teaching in Ioannina," whispered the people.

When Lascarina returned to Spetses after a long trip to the French port of Marseilles, she found that her stepfather had taken to his bed, weak from a persistent cough. Paraskevi, too, was exhausted.

"I am going to stay home for a while," Lascarina said to her mother, "to help you look after Lazarou."

"Are you sure Dimitri can spare you now?" asked Paraskevi.

Dimitri had been wandering through his in-laws' home, making repairs here and there. He smiled at Paraskevi's question and said, "I have not forgotten completely how to balance my books, although my crew may have to adjust to a grumpy captain." Then, seriously, he added, "With Lazarou sick and you so run down, Lascarina's place is here. And on top of that, we want our boys to start attending church. Plus, another baby is on the way."

"Yes," said Lascarina. "This spring."

And so, Lascarina helped Paraskevi and also learned from her how to run her own household. She supervised two cooks and two maids, in addition to the nanny, making sure her home was always well-provisioned and ready to welcome the many guests who would be passing through. The baby born in the spring was a girl and christened Eleni.

These days, instead of smirking at Lascarina behind her back, the villagers greeted her heartily and sent their children to meet her. The only person who never even acknowledged her presence was Popi. Lascarina knew Popi's taunt had triggered the events that led to her present happiness; she bore no grudges. But whenever she waved to the woman who had once tormented her, Popi would turn her head, pretending not to see Lascarina, her face reddening with lingering resentment and embarrassment. Popi now worked with her father, repairing shoes. Her husband was of little use, as he spent most of his time at the taverna, drinking.

One day, Lascarina met a boy who appeared to be ten years old. "Where are you learning your lessons?" she asked him. "Are you still at home or in Father Spiros's school?"

"Oh, Capitanissa!" said the boy, his eyes widening. "Did you not hear? A year ago, some soldiers came from Hydra and took Father Spiros away. They said it is now illegal for priests to teach. We haven't seen him since."

Lascarina grew pale. "I had thought that the priest we've been seeing in church was just standing in for Father Spiros, that Father Spiros had gone to visit his family in Nafplion."

The boy shook his head. "No, Father Spiros is *imprisoned* in the fortress at Nafplion. Father Andreas is our new priest, and he does not teach."

She confirmed the story with Paraskevi and Lazarou as soon as she saw them. "Yes," they said. "If the children learn to read at all these days, it is at home."

That night, Lascarina gazed at her own sleeping children and knew that she and Paraskevi could teach them. But what about the others? She could not drive from her mind the vision of the body dangling from the gallows, and she barely slept. Still, the next morning, she wrote a letter to Dimitri:

"My dear husband, I pray as always for your safe return. Please bring home twenty slates, five boxes of chalk, one hundred pencils, one hundred notebooks, twenty quill pens and inkwells, and three maps—one of Europe, one of the Ottoman Empire, and one of the world. Best if you wrap and hide these. Baby Eleni is starting to walk. We must bring her on at least one voyage. With all my love, Lascarina."

She gave the letter to a captain who was leaving Spetses that morning, letting him know the course Dimitri had planned: captains would exchange letters with one another in various ports, and many of these actually reached the intended recipient.

Dimitri did receive the message, for when he returned a month later, all the items Lascarina had requested were neatly packed in a trunk. She was delighted.

"Lascarina," asked Dimitri, "when you have a moment, could you please let me know what all this is about?"

Lascarina smiled. "Unless you have any objections, I am starting a school."

"A school? Where?"

"In our drawing room."

Dimitri looked at her in stunned silence for a moment and then burst into laughter. "And what do you think the *Bey* will think of that?"

"He wouldn't exactly approve, but why should he ever find out?" asked Lascarina.

"Good Heavens! Even Mustafa will notice that every day, several village children enter our house in the morning and stay for hours."

"Mustafa might very well notice…but he will hear that the children are being sent to work. We have a big house, right? Lots of cleaning, polishing, mending, cooking, children to look after…."

"Lascarina, what happened to Father Spiros?"

Lascarina's gaiety evaporated. Her stricken face told Dimitri what he needed to know.

"This is happening all over Greece," he said, grimly. "The yoke the Ottomans have placed upon us grows heavier by the week." He paced the floor. "I feel as if I am going to explode." He buried his face in his hands.

"I as well," said Lascarina softly. "But remember, we have our children, my parents, our friends, our servants…One misstep on our part, and we put them all in danger. We have to be ready this time before we strike." She stepped up to him, gently pulled his hands away from his face, and looked into his eyes. She saw in them a tormented, haunted look. "Dimitri, what is wrong?"

"I'm afraid I may have done something stupid," he said. "After leaving Marseilles, I sailed straight to Constantinople and filled out the usual paperwork, certifying that I was returning all the weapons I had borrowed from the armory. The *Porte* officials did not accept my attestation; they searched every inch of the ship, suspecting, it seems, that there were still arms hidden, that I was smuggling. Finally, they were satisfied. Then, instead of coming home, I sailed up to Odessa: Hypsilantis had sent a messenger to me, saying he wanted to meet."

Lascarina's heart skipped a beat: Alexander Hypsilantis was a fabulously wealthy Greek who lived in Constantinople but had been granted the title of "Prince" at the Russian court. In return for allowing him to retain his immense property, the Ottomans expected that he would maintain order in their provinces along the Danube River, Wallachia and Moldavia. Rumor had it that under the cover of "maintaining order," he was secretly organizing a revolutionary force.

"Dimitri," whispered Lascarina, "what did he want?"

"He wanted to borrow my ships. All six, other than the *Elpida*, were docked in Odessa, and they were all in good repair."

"Why?"

"I don't know for sure, but I can guess. He said only that he had some cargo that he needed to quickly transport up the Danube River. The ships were to be sailed by his own captains."

"What did you say?"

"Lascarina, I told him he could use the ships—I could not deny him. The Prince is in a position to help us when our time comes."

"But you did not sail yourself, correct?"

"Correct."

"So, we need to make this look as if it is just a business deal: you yourself did not sail, nor did you know what the ships were to carry. We can say that Hypsilantis rented your ships only to bring supplies up to his guards in Moldavia—and put a price on it."

With a somewhat calmer gaze, Dimitri regarded his wife. "I knew that I had married you for a reason. You are going to draw up a contract?"

Lascarina nodded.

"And I am going to ask Hypsilantis to sign it, seal it, and return it to me posthaste?"

Again Lascarina nodded. "He will realize that this should have been done straight away," she said. "That it is the only way to give you some cover. Now, what price should we ask?"

Dimitri thought a moment. "I think that, in a few years, one hundred thousand gold ducats might prove very useful."

Lascarina set to work immediately, writing through the night, knowing that the lives of all she held dear could depend on this document. The next morning, she handed it to Dimitri.

"One thing more," she said. "You yourself should not go again to Odessa to deliver this: the Turks know that you just returned from a long voyage. They will be suspicious."

"I will give it to Captain Stamos to carry," said Dimitri. "I would trust him with my life."

"Good," said Lascarina. "And to allay the *Porte's* suspicions even further, the Russian flag should be removed from our ships and perhaps at least four should be docked for now in Constantinople, where the Turks themselves can see them."

"Right again," said Dimitri, embracing his wife. "I will tell Stamos to hire Greek captains to sail the ships from Odessa to the *Porte.*"

When Hypsilantis read the contract, he knew that *not* having drafted such a document in the first place was a huge oversight. He had endangered Dimitri and all his family. He blanched a bit at the "rental fee," but signed. Within a fortnight, the sealed document was in Dimitri's hands.

Lascarina breathed a sigh of relief. "Now, what about the school?" she asked her husband.

"If I can loan our ships out to the mightiest gun-runner of them all," he said ruefully, "you can start a school."

Word of Lascarina's classroom spread throughout Spetses. Soon, eight children, aged seven to twelve, trudged each morning to her house. Always, if asked, they said they were doing errands of various sorts. Lascarina mostly taught arithmetic, while Paraskevi and Lazarou tutored them in reading, writing and history. Of course, the children learned about ancient Athens and Sparta, but they also studied the Byzantine Empire, the Greek Empire that lasted for a thousand years until it fell to the Ottoman Turks in 1453. Their teachers reminded them that, because the last Byzantine Emperor had died without surrendering, he inspired his people to carry on their resistance against the Ottomans.

Peter, the boy who had told Lascarina about the arrest of Father Spiros, raised his hand. "Capitanissa," he asked, "the map with the Sultan's seal shows the 'Greek Provinces' as being just the Peloponnesus and the islands close by, like ours. But the map you drew of Greek lands in the Byzantine Empire shows them stretching all the way north, to Epirus and Thessaly, and east to Smyrna. Are you saying that *all* the people on your map are Greek?"

"Absolutely," said Lascarina. "We are one people, whether we are furriers in the north, fishermen and traders on the islands, bankers in Constantinople, or farmers on the mainland. All of us are forced to pay tribute to—and serve—the Sultan. We will never again be free unless we work together. We've seen what happens when we don't."

A Darkening Sky

The winter of 1811, Dimitri remained on Spetses. A series of storms, more violent than had ever been seen, roiled the Mediterranean and Black Seas, forcing him to cancel his voyages. He took the opportunity to have his three ships in Spetses re-caulked and fitted with new rigging.

One gray morning in January, the quiet of Lascarina's classroom was shattered by the sound of running footsteps. Peter's younger sister came pounding into the drawing room, her eyes filled with terror. "Capitanissa," she cried, "the *Bey* is here, the *Bey* from Hydra! He went to find Captain Bouboulis on his ship—he is there speaking with him now."

Lascarina froze. The Ottoman Governor of the Saronic islands usually stayed in his fortress on Hydra. What had brought him to Spetses? Why was he speaking with her husband? What if he came to the house? Lascarina drew a deep breath. "Children," she said, "take your jackets and run home, but through the woods, not along the docks." The children fled the room. Lascarina tore down the maps that had been pinned to the walls and Lazarou burned them in the hearth outside. Paraskevi ran out a back door, her arms laden with slates, papers and pencils. No sooner had she left than Dimitri and the *Bey* entered the courtyard, followed by ten guards from the *Bey's* flagship.

"Lascarina," said Dimitri, his brow furrowed but his voice calm, "the *Bey* wants to search our house."

The *Bey*, a tall, stout man, wore a red turban and a heavily embroidered, fur-lined robe over a white tunic. He looked around the drawing room, examining the furniture, paintings, and carpets. "Quite a nice place you have here, Captain," he said, completely ignoring Lascarina. He smiled thinly and peered at Dimitri: "I wonder where you found the money to build such a nice place."

"Go ahead—search!" he ordered his soldiers. The guards opened cabinets and cupboards and looked under beds and benches. "There seems to be nothing here, Sir," said one of them to the *Bey*.

"Tap on the walls, then! They probably have some tunnels." The *Bey's* long brown beard seemed to quiver with the excitement of the hunt.

Gradually Lascarina's heart stopped pounding as she saw the soldiers overlook the small shreds of evidence that pointed to the existence of her classroom. She could contain herself no longer. "What on earth are you looking for?" she asked.

"What do you think, woman? Guns!" shouted the *Bey*. "*Smuggled* guns. We have been briefed by the *Porte* on your husband's extensive trade with our Russian friends and the naval fleet he is building."

Dimitri's eyes flashed. "Didn't the *Porte* officials let you know that I have spent countless hours in their offices, answering their questions? My ships have been searched from stem to stern. *Nothing* other than what I described in my cargo statements was ever found. And has the *Porte* observed a single frigate among my 'naval fleet'? My ships are for trade, not war!"

The *Bey* ignored Dimitri's outburst. For two hours, his soldiers combed through every crevice of the house, from cellar to attic, checking whether walls were solid and peering behind furniture for secret doors. Lascarina and Dimitri sat in silence.

"Well," the *Bey* said finally to Dimitri, "you are lucky. Had we found weapons, we would have hanged you this evening. As it is, we will just bring you back with us to Hydra and hold you there until the *Emir* tells me how your subversion will be punished."

Dimitri started. "What do you mean, my 'subversion'?"

"Oh, come now…You can't imagine that the *Porte* is unaware that you transported guns for the Russians up to the Danubian Provinces?"

"That is not true," said Dimitri, coolly now, "and I can prove it." He took the contract Hypsilantis had signed out of his desk drawer and showed it to the *Bey*. "You can read for yourself that Prince Hypsilantis *rented* my ships. They were captained by his own men for that trip, and I have no idea what they transported."

The *Bey* read the contract carefully and then fixed a cold stare on Dimitri. "Well, it appears that the *Emir* is not aware of this. I will let him know—he can question Hypsilantis himself." He remained silent for a few minutes, and again his lips curved into a thin smile. "We will give you a good opportunity to demonstrate your loyalty to the Sultan. I know that the *Emir* needs to have some grain delivered to a distant outpost, and you are the perfect captain for the job."

"From where will the grain be collected," asked Dimitri, "and to where does it have to be taken?"

"From our silos in Salonika to our troops in Alexandria."

Dimitri and Lascarina exchanged glances. Both knew that the waters around the Egyptian port of Alexandria were infested with pirates.

"I assume," said Lascarina, "that you will provide my husband with a military escort?"

The *Bey* looked at her with disdain. "You assume wrongly. Do you think we can spare any of our ships for military escorts these days?"

"You know very well that the Egyptian coast is even more treacherous than Gibraltar," hissed Lascarina fiercely.

"Yes, that is why your husband is so well-qualified for this job. We are aware of how often he has triumphed in his skirmishes with pirates." The *Bey* turned to Dimitri. "You may borrow two additional cannons from our armory on Hydra for this trip, and, as usual, you will be allowed to carry enough long guns and pistols for your crew. You are to set sail within the fortnight. Do you understand me?"

Again Dimitri and Lascarina looked at one another. Dimitri's refusal to undertake this mission would provide the Ottomans with an excuse to arrest him.

"I understand you quite well," said Dimitri quietly.

With that, the *Bey* turned on his heel and marched his soldiers out of the house. He was pleased: the *Emir* would reward him handsomely, he thought, for having found a captain to make this perilous trip.

The despair that Dimitri saw in Lascarina's eyes pierced his heart. "We must not give up," he said. "You saw that your contract saved me."

Lascarina shook her head. "No, it wasn't your deal with the Russians that bothered them. They just tried to use that as an excuse to seize our fleet. They are crumbling," she said bitterly. "They are desperate for money, however they can find it, and ships."

"Yes," said Dimitri. "One more battle with pirates will just limber me up to fight *them*."

Tears came to Lascarina's eyes. "I want to go with you," she said softly.

"Darling, you know that is impossible. Our children and your parents need you. Spetses needs you."

Yiannis, Georgios and even the toddler, Eleni, sensed that their father's next voyage would be much more dangerous than usual. Dimitri spent as much time as he could with them, even letting them stay with him and Lascarina as they tried to map out the safest route to Alexandria.

The ship he would use for this trip was as fast as the *Capitanissa* and as sturdy as the *Elpida*. Dimitri offered high pay, but finding a crew this time was not easy.

Harry, his trusty first mate, was willing to accompany him.

"No, Harry," said Dimitri. "You must remain here, on Spetses. The Capitanissa may need your help."

Harry nodded, fully understanding what Dimitri meant. "Yes, Captain, I know. Rest easy. Should the need arise, I will serve her with the same devotion as I would my own sister."

Word of Dimitri's assignment spread throughout Spetses. On the day of his departure, all the islanders gathered at the harbor where Father Andreas led them in a prayer for his safe return. Though Lascarina kept her voice from cracking as she bid her husband farewell, she could not keep tears from welling in her eyes. Dimitri gathered her in his arms and kissed her.

"Promise me," he said, "that whatever happens, you will keep the flame of freedom burning in the hearts of our children."

"I promise," she said.

Three weeks after Dimitri set sail, Lascarina received a letter that he had written in Salonika—then, two weeks later, one from Crete, the Greek island farthest south in the Mediterranean, closest to Egypt. Day after day, she waited for further word. Her heart grew increasingly heavy.

Five months after Dimitri left, a ship from Crete dropped anchor in Spetses's harbor. Its captain mentioned to one of the dockhands a ferocious battle he had seen some distance off the Egyptian coast.

"Was this near Alexandria?" asked the dockhand sharply.

"Why yes," said the Captain. "How did you guess?"

"It's a long story," said the dockhand, grabbing him by the arm. "Come with me to the Capitanissa's house. You must tell her what you saw."

In Lascarina's presence, the captain from Crete bowed. "Madame," he said, "I am told you have some interest in a battle I witnessed off Alexandria?"

"Yes," said Lascarina, all color draining from her face.

"Very well then. About four months ago, as I myself was dodging Barbary pirates on my way to that city, I chanced to see from some distance a merchant ship set upon by two corsairs. They easily carried twenty cannons each, those corsairs. The captain of the barque fought like a devil. He scored a direct hit on one of the corsairs, and it sank before my eyes. From my spyglass, I saw the captain fall on deck, bleeding from a wound to the chest."

Bouboulina sank into a chair and a sob rose from her heart. "The captain of that merchant ship was my husband." Slowly and with many pauses to collect herself, she told the visitor of Dimitri's forced journey to Alexandria.

"My greatest sympathy, Madame. Your husband was obviously a brilliant and brave captain. And," he added slowly, "one who valued the lives of his men. Just before he fell, I saw him gesture toward the ship's rowboat: clearly he was ordering his crew to abandon ship. They moved to lift him but he shook his head and motioned for them to go quickly. They rowed away like mad. I'll wager they all reached safety. The pirates climbed on board, saw the captain lying dead, stole whatever they wanted from his quarters—they were not interested in grain—and shot a volley of cannon balls into the splintering ship so that she sank quickly."

Bouboulina wept. Her dear husband, her friend, the love of her life...could not even be buried. His body lay in the sea off the coast of Egypt. She looked up at the visitor and, through her tears, murmured, "Better to have heard this news from you than from the Turks. Thank you."

In those first terrible weeks after receiving word of Dimitri's death, Bouboulina focused whatever strength she could muster on comforting her children, trying to find the words to explain to them how and why their father had died. Two months later, her heart still heavy as lead, she summoned to Spetses all the men who had captained Dimitri's ships or served on his crews, to confirm what they had long dreaded.

"Madame Bouboulis," asked one of the captains Dimitri had hired just the previous year, "now that the Captain is gone, when will you sell the ships?"

The men who had known Dimitri and Bouboulina for a longer time looked at one another and smiled: they knew what she would answer.

"Sell our ships?" repeated Bouboulina, dumbfounded. "That is not my plan at all. I will be continuing my husband's business. I called you here today to pay any outstanding debts Dimitri owed you, and to ask those of you who would like to keep working with me to convene here again four weeks from today. At that time, I will assign you your new jobs."

Bouboulina sought out the merchants for whom Dimitri had transported goods and managed to convince almost all of them to continue doing business with her. In a month's time, the Bouboulis ships were once again laden with cargo, their captains plying familiar routes and venturing into new ports as well.

One morning, a year after her first meeting with the captains, Bouboulina sat in the study, reviewing her new accounts. For the first time in months, her heart felt lighter—Dimitri would have been proud to see his business thrive. Suddenly, her maid burst into the room. "Capitanissa," she cried, "some Ottoman official was pounding at the door. I let him into the parlor." She trembled with fear. "This one isn't from Hydra," she said.

Bouboulina's hands shook. She took a deep breath and strode into the parlor. The official standing before her was a short, scrawny man, but as soon as she saw the insignia on his oversized robe, she knew he represented the Sultan. He had come from Constantinople.

"Who are you?" she demanded.

The little man drew himself up. "Ahmad, secretary to the Sultan's Minister of Finance."

"What do you want?"

"Madame, you are ordered to pay a fine of ten thousand gold ducats and to surrender to us six of your late husband's ships."

The secretary unfurled a scroll and thrust it toward Bouboulina. She gasped as she read the charges against her, and her eyes blazed. "Is it not enough for your Minister that my husband is dead? Must he also make beggars of us?"

"If your husband had not died in that pirate attack, we would at this moment be arresting him," barked the secretary, even as he backed out the front door, away from Bouboulina, "for we have *incontrovertible* evidence that Bouboulis was involved in a Russian plot against our Sultan."

"You fool!" said Bouboulina. "The *Bey* from Hydra told the *Emir* about the contract Dimitri had with Prince Hypsilantis—he was *not* collaborating with the Russians."

"I can assure you, Madame, that the Minister of Finance couldn't care less about what any *Emir* heard about any contract your husband might have signed with any Russian prince."

Bouboulina longed with all her heart to grab one of the vases in her salon and break it over the intruder's head. *Never* would she give in to this demand! But flying into a rage now would get her nowhere. She needed time, if only a day, to make a plan. "I must determine how I can comply most quickly with your request," she said to the secretary.

"Very well. I shall expect you to have your affairs in order by tomorrow morning when I depart for Constantinople to report to my Minister on this matter." With that, the secretary turned and left, swaying a bit under his heavy robe.

Bouboulina's thoughts raced. She would have to go to Constantinople herself to petition the Minister of Finance directly. Negotiating with his underling here would get her nowhere. She sent her maid to fetch Paraskevi and Soula. As she hurriedly packed her trunk, she explained to them what had happened.

Soula was appalled, sure that her friend was making a terrible mistake. "Your children have already lost their father. Are they to lose their mother as well? You must not go! Who can help you there? They may imprison you, kill you. Even if they seize your ships, you will still have your house and land."

"Yes," said Bouboulina. "And what is to stop them from coming next year to demand those too? Moreover, I cannot support the school without some income. And our children must be prepared, first to fight and then to govern themselves."

Bouboulina sat on top of the half-packed trunk, Paraskevi and Soula on either side of her, and buried her face in her hands. All of a sudden, she felt so very tired. Where would she find the strength for this voyage? She sobbed as the tears she had dammed up for so many months rolled down her face. Soula's heart sank, for she had never seen her friend cry like this.

Paraskevi put her arms around her daughter's shoulders. "You will be surprised," she whispered, "to see how strong you are." For some moments, Paraskevi gazed into the distance, remembering her own desperate journey to Constantinople. "Dimitri had powerful friends in Constantinople. They can help you. You should go."

Silently, Paraskevi and Soula helped Bouboulina finish packing. The next morning, she met the secretary at the dock. Following her were two servants carrying her trunk. The secretary's eyes widened. Had this woman loaded all her gold into that trunk?

"I will not be able to pay the fine with what my husband left me here in Spetses," Bouboulina announced. "He did his banking in Constantinople, and two of our ships are still docked there. I must draw upon those resources to meet the demands of the Minister of Finance."

The secretary was stupefied. "You...You mean to return to Constantinople with me?"

"Yes. Unless you care to explain to your Minister why you were unable to comply with his order."

The clerk had no desire whatsoever to do such a thing. Better to bring the woman along, just as she suggested, so the *effendi*, his boss, could question her for himself.

They sailed away on the Ottoman frigate. Ahead, the skies were a dark, leaden gray. Bouboulina turned and stared back at Spetses, as if to fix its pine forests and whitewashed homes in her memory forever.

VII

The Russian Ambassador and the *Valide Sultan*

The widow and her traveling companion exchanged not one word during the five-day voyage to Constantinople. They ate their meals in silence and avoided walking on the deck at the same time. Bouboulina plotted her strategy. Her mother was right: Dimitri did have many wealthy and powerful friends in Constantinople. Most important among them was the Russian ambassador to the *Porte*, Stroganov. *He* could verify to the Minister of Finance that her husband had not been involved in any conspiracy. But she would need to see him quickly. How could she get around the diplomatic protocols that stood in the way of a face–to–face meeting?

They reached the waters of the Golden Horn. Stretching for miles before them was the city of Constantinople. Hundreds of minarets pierced the sky. Rising in their midst was the great dome of Hagia Sophia. The inside of what once had been the greatest basilica in Christendom was now desolate and ruined; gone were the mosaics that had sparkled in the glow of a thousand candles, gone were the gilded icons—the paintings of saints—that had inspired the prayers of the faithful. No services had been sung there since the one attended by Emperor Constantine, who immediately afterward led his troops into their final battle against the Ottoman invaders and died with them on the city ramparts. Suddenly Bouboulina thought of the one man who could bring her immediately to Stroganov: Patriarch Grigorius.

"We are to meet with the Minister of Finance tomorrow, precisely at noon," said the secretary as they docked.

"I will be there," said Bouboulina. "Today, I am calling upon His Holiness, Patriarch Grigorius."

"You had better be there," growled the secretary. "If you are not, you *and* your dear Holiness will be thrown into the Sultan's dungeon."

Bouboulina shuddered at the thought of sharing her father's fate—and of bringing it upon the Patriarch. This was no empty threat. Whenever the Sultan was vexed with his Orthodox Christian subjects, he would vent his anger on the leader of their church.

Bouboulina found two porters to carry her trunk. They led her to the old Greek quarter, where sagging wooden balconies of two- and three-story houses overhung narrow, crooked streets and cast them in shadows. The milling crowd threatened to separate her from her porters. Bouboulina could scarcely hear herself think above the babel of tongues. Finally, they found the Patriarchate, a decrepit stone and timber building not much different from the others.

"Please, let His Holiness know that the widow of Captain Dimitri Bouboulis needs *urgently* to see him," she said to the servant at the front door.

Within a few minutes, the Patriarch appeared, standing tall in his black robes, a *skufia*, or black cap, perched on his head. With his long white beard and intense dark eyes, he could himself have stepped out of an icon.

"Madame Bouboulis," said the Patriarch. "I knew your husband; he would call on me whenever he stayed in this city. I heard of his death. It is sad indeed that such a fine young man met an untimely end at the hands of pirates."

"Your Holiness, we think that his death did not happen entirely by chance." Bouboulina quickly recounted the events of the past months. "I am determined not to surrender our estate," she concluded. "I think that Ambassador Stroganov could help me, if only he will see me today."

"When is your audience with the Minister of Finance?"

"Tomorrow at noon."

"Then we have not a moment to lose! We must find Stroganov at once."

Patriarch Grigorius led the way to the Russian Consulate, a colonnaded marble mansion overlooking the Bosphorus Strait, and asked that the Ambassador be summoned immediately. Soon Stroganov appeared, a tall, suave aristocrat. His receding hairline accentuated an already prominent forehead and wire-rimmed spectacles magnified his intensely blue eyes. He moved with an ease that showed him to be completely at home in the glittering and mirrored splendor of the Tsar's embassy.

"Madame Bouboulis!" he said. "The Captain often speaks of you. What a pleasure to finally meet you in person."

"You do not know that my husband was killed?"

"No! How terrible!" Stroganov's distress seemed genuine enough. "When? How?"

As Bouboulina again told her story, Stroganov listened, leaning against a wall with his arms folded across his chest, head bowed, eyes almost closed. He was accustomed to hearing tales of woe. When she finished, he looked at her intently, just for an instant; with that practiced glance, he had learned to peer through the facades of even the most sophisticated diplomats. His well-honed instinct told him that this woman spoke the truth.

"For once," he said, "I can swear in good faith that an acquaintance of mine had no part in any conspiracy. Your husband's dealings in Odessa were purely commercial—he loved you and his children too much to put you in danger. Although," and here the Ambassador's eyes twinkled, "I must say the price you put on the transaction with Hypsilantis was quite high." Stroganov's face became serious again and his voice grim as he continued: "The Turks' charges are groundless, but I must warn you that the Minister you will meet tomorrow is among the most greedy and unreasonable officials in the Sultan's court."

Just then, a secretary rushed in with a note for the Ambassador. "Excuse me," said Stroganov, "I have an appointment. I will see you tomorrow at the Ministry, at noon."

The next morning, Patriarch Grigorius guided Bouboulina to the Ministry of Finance, a massive and unattractive building in Constantinople's new administrative center. Stopping some distance from the outermost gate, he said, "Here I must leave you. It will not help your case to be seen with me."

To Bouboulina's relief, Stroganov was waiting at the entrance to the Ministry. She had not been entirely sure that he would keep his word. They walked through one large hall after another, each filled with scores of desks, at which clerks sat laboring behind piles of documents. Finally, they reached the audience chamber. Inside, cowering before his *effendi*, was Ahmad, the secretary.

The Minister of Finance was seated on a dais in the center of the huge chamber. He wore a black silk caftan and a scarlet fez. On several of his fingers were rings set with rubies and emeralds. He peered down at Bouboulina and Stroganov, his face haughty. "So," he said, "you are Lascarina Bouboulis, wife of the late Captain?"

"Yes."

"Then you will now pay the fine and sign over your ships."

"No."

"What?" The Minister scowled in disbelief, first at Bouboulina and then at his secretary.

Sweat poured down Ahmad's face. He seemed to have trouble breathing. "But…but that is why you came with me to Constantinople," he gasped.

"I came to Constantinople to present my case in person to the Minister of Finance! Your charge that my husband was a traitor is groundless. Ambassador Stroganov is here with me to…"

"I can well imagine why Stroganov is here!" roared the minister. "If you think I would accept the word of the Tsar's Ambassador—or of the Russian puppet, Hypsilantis—over that of our most trusted spies, you are a complete idiot!"

"Really now, Rahman, this is unseemly," said Stroganov, wincing at such an undiplomatic show of temper.

"Let's not stand on protocol, Stroganov! If she does not pay the fine and surrender the ships by the end of the week, she'll be hanged—just as Bouboulis should have been!" The Minister whirled around to face his secretary. "And you too!" he shouted. "What do you mean, wasting my time like this?"

He stormed out the door. Ahmad fainted. Stroganov took Bouboulina by the arm and led her outside. She started to weep from exhaustion and disappointment. Stroganov was non-plussed—a rare experience for him. First a temper tantrum, then fainting, and now tears. What a mess! "There, there," he said to Bouboulina. "Don't give up yet. We have one more card left to play."

"What on earth is that?"

"The *Valide Sultan*, Nakshidil."

"The Sultan's *mother*?" Bouboulina stared at the Ambassador through her tears. The *Valide Sultan* was kept locked in the harem, along with the Sultan's wives and concubines. What could she know about these matters?

"Yes. *She* is the real power behind Mahmud's throne. The Sultan is off on a hunting trip now—somewhere in the Danubian provinces, the lucky dog—and he has left the reins of government in her hands."

"But how did you even meet the Valide Nakshidil?"

"Oh, of course, we have never met in person. We communicate through messengers. They say she is still quite beautiful." For a moment, Stroganov looked wistful, and then he chuckled. "The old lady loves a bit of intrigue now and then. And well she might. She's survived plenty of conspiracies in her time and managed to get her youngest son on the throne to boot!"

"Her *youngest* son?" Bouboulina was puzzled, as this was not the usual order of succession.

"Yes. The older two were poisoned by other harem women who entertained ambitions for their own offspring."

"Ugh! This Empire is rotten to the core."

"So says the Tsar as well. But rotten or not, the *Valide Sultan* is your only hope."

Stroganov summoned his sumptuous crimson carriage. Emblazoned in gold on its door was the Russian imperial eagle. "Topkapi," he said to the driver. The carriage passed from the straight, dull streets of the government quarter into a vast open plaza. Ahead lay the brick fortifications that surrounded Topkapi Palace.

"The walls are endless!" said Bouboulina.

"Sultan Mahmud's palace is a small city," said Stroganov. "Behind those walls live over one thousand courtiers and guards, at least three thousand servants and slaves, and who knows how many harem women."

They stopped outside the audience hall. Stroganov spoke to the guard: "Kindly let the *Valide Sultan* know that the Russian Ambassador entreats her to hear an urgent request from one of his personal friends, a Greek lady." The guard nodded. This was not the first time he had relayed messages to the *Valide* from the Russian Ambassador.

"What could Stroganov be up to now?" wondered Nakshidil, when she received the message. At least she could count on the wily Ambassador to make her day a little more interesting. "Send her in," she said. "I will speak with her here, in the harem."

"The *Valide Sultan* will see you," said the guard to Bouboulina.

He led her through gardens bursting with yellow, orange and red tulips—tulips with frilled petals, unlike any she had ever seen. Carefully tended flowering jasmine vines climbed the walls; the air was heavy with their scent. Peacocks strutted along the paths, and songbirds flitted through the trees. At last they reached the shadowy arches of the harem's portico, where they were met by a woman veiled in black from head to toe. She peered through a slit in the scarf that covered her face.

"Come with me," she said in Greek. "I am the *Valide's* slave."

Bouboulina's eyes widened as she entered the harem. Delicately carved ivory screens partitioned a huge room. Brilliant crimson and blue Persian carpets were strewn over marble floors. Plump velvet cushions stood stacked around ebony tables. Tiles painted with designs of exotic flowers—all in turquoise, white, green and red—covered the walls.

"I feel as if I am looking through a kaleidoscope," thought Bouboulina.

Safe here from the eyes of men, the harem women wandered about unveiled, in silken caftans and voluminous trousers. Strings of gold beads and jewels hung casually about their necks and pearls studded their hair. They stared at this visitor from the outside world.

"Here is the Valide Nakshidil," the slave announced. Bouboulina had not noticed the petite blond woman standing in the shadows of an arch. For a moment, she stared. The *Valide* was only slightly older than Bouboulina. Her pale blue caftan was embroidered with pearls, and mounted in her diadem was an enormous emerald that had once belonged to the Byzantine Empress Theodora. Despite Nakshidil's seeming fragility, her bearing was regal and her gaze, imperious. Her lips wore a quizzical smile, but her deep set blue eyes were ever watchful.

Recovering her wits, Bouboulina said to the servant, "I don't speak Turkish. Can you translate?"

"That will not be necessary," said Nakshidil, in perfect Greek.

Bouboulina started. "This woman must have been stolen from a Greek family," she thought.

The *Valide Sultan* had observed this reaction many times before. "It's not quite as you imagine," she said drily. "My parents were peasants near Salonika with seven children to feed, six of them boys. They sold *me* to our local *pasha* when I was eleven. Recognizing my value, the *pasha* sent me here. I have no great love for the land of my birth. Tell me why you are here."

"My husband was wrongfully accused of collaborating with the Russians."

"So he was hanged?"

"No, he was ordered to undertake a voyage that brought him into dangerous waters, where he was killed by pirates."

"How convenient," said Nakshidil. "He must have been quite rich." Bouboulina glared at her. "Well," continued the *Valide Sultan*, unfazed, "now what?"

"Now they want to confiscate a large part of my husband's estate. Who knows where their demands will end! I will not be able to support our children."

"And you realize that you yourself could be executed for contesting this order?"

"I have no choice. I will not let my family be driven into the ground."

Nakshidil sat silently for a few moments, her eyes darkened by unspeakably sad memories. When she finally spoke, her voice was weary. "You may not believe this, but I too once risked everything for my children." She turned to her slave. "Alev, bring me paper and ink."

She wrote a brief message, sealed it, and handed it to the slave. "Have the guard deliver this today to the *Grand Vizier*." Then she turned to Bouboulina. "I assume you're staying at the Patriarchate. Go back there. This evening, the *Grand Vizier* will have a word with the Minister of Finance. Tomorrow morning, a document will be delivered to you. It will bear the signature of the Minister of Finance as well as the seal of the Sultan himself and will permit you to retain all your property."

Bouboulina gasped. "How can I ever thank you?"

"Our *beys* in the Greek provinces tell us that rebellion is brewing."

Bouboulina looked at the *Valide Sultan* with apprehension. How much did she know?

"Oh, maybe not in a backwater like Spetses," continued Nakshidil dismissively, "but certainly in the North. As you well know, thousands of Turkish families live in Greece. Many have been there over three hundred years. Innocent Turks—

women and children—stand to be slaughtered by your vengeful countrymen."

Inwardly Bouboulina cringed, knowing full well that over the past few months, her heart had been filled with hatred. Could such hatred lead to murder, she wondered?

"Yes," continued the *Valide Sultan* grimly, "your revolution will not be a pretty thing. Remember me when you have the chance to save innocent lives."

"I will," said Bouboulina. She bowed to Nakshidil and quickly left the harem, following the path through the garden. Yes, it was all quite beautiful, but the scent of jasmine grew cloying. The Sultan's pleasure palace was, after all, no more than a gilded cage. It was a relief to stand free in the open air.

The next morning, Bouboulina held in her hands the *ferman*, the decree from the Minister of Finance that allowed her to keep her ships. There, at the bottom, proving that the document was genuine, was the seal of the Sultan. Now she could go home.

"Will you be leaving your two ships here?" asked the Patriarch as they stood in his small study.

"No," said Bouboulina. "I will sail one home myself, but I need to find a captain for the other, someone from here who can hire crews for both ships."

"Yes, it would be advisable for you to keep a close watch on your property. Is there anything else you need besides a captain for your ship?"

"I will be eternally grateful for all the help you've given me already. There is, though," said Bouboulina hesitantly, "a visit I'd like to make, since I am here."

"Yes?"

"I would like to go to the cemetery. My father is buried there."

"Who was your father?"

"Stavrianos Pinotsis."

"Kyra Bouboulis," said the Patriarch with a smile, "it seems that revolution runs in your veins." He continued slowly: "No one knows better than I that while we live under our Ottoman overlords, we have no freedom. Our lives depend on their whims—churches open, churches closed, taxes on paper, taxes on ink. Remember, though, that when your rebellion breaks out—as we know it will—the Greeks of Constantinople will pay heavily. Remember, always, that war is an abomination."

There was a knock at the door of the Patriarch's study. "Father Constantinou?" called the Patriarch.

The door opened, and a silver-haired priest poked his head in.

"Come in, Father. I know I am late for my appointment. I am leaving now. Please help Kyra Bouboulis here—she would like to visit a grave in our cemetery."

"I would be glad to take her," said Father Constantinou.

"And, Father," added the Patriarch, with the trace of a smile, "I think you may also be able to help her with another problem. She needs to hire a captain. If I recall correctly, you belong to some society where she might meet a few trustworthy candidates, yes?"

"Um, yes," said Father Constantinou.

"And there is a meeting this evening?"

"Yes."

"Perfect," said the Patriarch, and left for his appointment.

A Resourceful Society

F ather Constantinou strode through the narrow streets, leading Bouboulina to the old Christian cemetery at the outskirts of the Greek quarter. "For whose grave are you searching?" he asked.

"My father's, Stavrianos Pinotsis."

The priest stared at her. "Stavrianos Pinotsis! It was I who gave him the last rites—and who christened you!" he exclaimed. "I had just been ordained as a priest then, in 1771."

"I was with your father when he died," Father Constantinou continued. "His last words were about you and your mother, how much he loved you, how much he hoped you would live to see freedom."

The priest knew exactly where to find the grave. Bouboulina read the dates of her father's birth and death on his headstone and felt a now-familiar ache in her heart. He was just thirty years old when he died.

She and Father Constantinou left the cemetery in silence. After Bouboulina had walked a bit, she was able to speak again. "I want to return home quickly, to tell my mother that I met you and that I saw my father's grave. His Holiness mentioned that you belonged to a society that might help me recruit a captain," she said. "Would you mind telling me where to find this group?"

The priest looked troubled. Finally he spoke, hesitantly. "Yes, I do belong to a society. Frankly, I was surprised the Patriarch knew not only that I had joined but that there was a meeting tonight. The organization was formed just six months ago. If the Turks ever find out about it, they will hunt down each and every member and kill him—we do not want to expose the Patriarch to additional danger. He is in enough already."

"So," said Bouboulina slowly, "this society must have something to do with our fight for freedom."

Father Constantinou nodded. "I can bring you to tonight's meeting only if you are sure that, no matter what happens, you will not reveal who you have seen there."

Bouboulina felt her heart sink. She had already been through one ordeal. Could she stand more? "Planning this revolution," she thought, "is going to take every ounce of my strength. Can I do it?" They were almost back at the Patriarchate before she turned to Father Constantinou and said, "Yes. I am sure."

The priest nodded. "The meeting will be held after nightfall. I will meet you here at eight. We will go together."

Just before she left her room to join the priest, Bouboulina tucked the decree from the Minister of Finance into her vest; the captain she would try to recruit might want to see proof that it was safe to sail her ship away from the *Porte*. Once more, Father Constantinou led Bouboulina through tortuous streets and alleys, this time to his home, a ramshackle, unkempt building with boards nailed over the cellar windows and a balcony hanging loose, swaying with every breeze. "This is where you were born, Kyra Bouboulis. Of course, it was a tidy, pretty house back then, when your mother and uncle came to stay, and my sister was alive. But it better serves our purpose now for it to look abandoned."

The rickety wooden stairway creaked as they descended to the cellar. Someone was already inside, for when Father Constantinou whispered a password, the door swung open, groaning on its rusty hinges. A few dark figures hovered near a shaded lantern. Bouboulina picked out three familiar faces: Captains Apostolis and Kanaris, friends of Dimitri from the far-off island of Psara, and Germanos, the fiery and wily bishop of Patras who had so far managed to elude the many Ottoman henchmen who had been sent to capture him. The rest of the men seemed to be from Constantinople and Smyrna. Quickly Father Constantinou introduced Bouboulina and explained that she needed to hire a captain; the company, already aware of Dimitri's death, accepted the presence of Bouboulina, for they knew that the widow of their gallant friend would never betray them.

The silence outside was broken by a muffled rapping on boards covering a rear window: two slow taps and three quick. Through the shadows, Bouboulina discerned the outline of a second entrance to the cellar, a trap door opposite the one through which she had entered. Germanos sprang to unbolt it.

In strode Petrobey Mavromichaelis and Theodoros Kolokotronis, followed by four of their warriors. The *armatoloi* were not wearing their white kilts now. They were disguised in clerical robes. Clearly uncomfortable and unaccustomed to the need for silence, they tried clumsily to stifle the banging of daggers and pistols hidden under their robes. They remained huddled near the door, eyeing the others with suspicion. Bouboulina remembered Lazarou's prediction that their stronghold in Mani would be the cradle of Greek independence. "I hope they can learn how to work with the rest of us," she thought nervously.

"Praise God," cried Germanos to Kolokotronis and Mavromichaelis, "you made it! Did you know the Turks have put a price of five thousand ducats on your heads?"

"I'm not sure they would recognize our heads anymore," said Kolokotronis, whose long hair, like Mavromichaelis's, had turned white years ago. "But good to know they think they're still worth it."

The *armatoloi* were persuaded to join the rest of the company just as the guest of honor mounted a makeshift podium. It was Dimitri Hypsilantis, a general in the Russian army and nephew of the man who had borrowed Dimitri's ships. Alexander, the older Hypsilantis, had been beheaded by the Ottomans just recently, as his fellow conspirators, who had been tracked down in Moldavia, confessed under torture that he was financing the formation of a revolutionary force; his title as a Russian prince had offered no protection. "This family," thought Bouboulina, "has already suffered greatly for freedom, despite their wealth and high position." The Russian military medals on young Hypsilantis's uniform glittered in the flickering candlelight.

"My fellow patriots," he began, "now is the time for us to recruit new members to our Society of Friends, the *Philiki Eteria*. We must put aside our differences and stand together for a common cause." Forgetting the need for quiet, his audience applauded. "For do not deceive yourselves," Hypsilantis continued, "when battle is joined, you will have only yourselves to rely upon." Kolokotronis nodded in agreement. "Leaders of Austria and Germany tremble at the thought of any challenge to the existing order, and our Tsar, devoted as he is to Orthodoxy, is no friend of Revolution. We, my friends, will pose exactly...."

Hypsilantis fell silent, for suddenly all heard the sound of footsteps—tens of footsteps—marching down the deserted street. Father Constantinou turned white as a sheet and gestured for all to exit through the trap door. One glance from Kolokotronis's eagle eyes told his own men to obey. He stood by the door to help the others leave. "I am staying with Father Constantinou," breathed Bouboulina. "I have a plan. I need just one captain from Constantinople to remain with us."

That Kolokotronis had survived to old age was a credit to his sharp instincts. Based on those, he made life-and-death decisions on the spot. Now, he decided he could trust this woman. "All right," he whispered. "Captain Istianou, will you stay?"

"Yes," murmured Istianou, who was as pale as Father Constantinou.

"My lady," said Kolokotronis to Bouboulina, as he himself turned to leave, "we will be hiding right outside the door. If you need us, scream."

Bouboulina nodded, doubting at this moment that she was capable of even a squeak. She, the priest and the captain hurriedly removed the podium from its base, turned it into a table, and sat around it. "If you have a map," said Bouboulina, "lay it on the table." With shaking hands, Istianou did so. At that moment, many fists started pounding on the front door. Father Constantinou breathed a quick prayer and, just as the door started to tear off its hinges, opened it.

Twenty Ottoman guards burst in, scimitars raised, their blood-curdling shouts echoing into the street. "You're all under arrest," shouted their sergeant. He peered through the shadows. Aside from the priest who let them in, the cellar held only two figures at a table, one of them a woman. "Search the place!" he ordered his men.

Bouboulina's heart skipped a beat as they tried to push open the trap door, but clearly Kolokotronis had some of his soldiers standing on it: it would not budge. "That hasn't been opened in twenty years," said Father Constantinou.

"All right," growled the officer. "What's going on here? Where are the rest of you?"

"It's just us," said Bouboulina, speaking slowly and steadily, despite her pounding heart. "I came to Father Constantinou's house to hire Captain Istianou here to sail one of my ships back to my island, Spetses."

"A likely story," scoffed the officer. "This decrepit place can't be anyone's home."

"Actually," said Father Constantinou calmly, "it's mine. I have lived here for forty–five years. Since my dear sister died, I've been unable to tend to it properly. I can show you upstairs, but I must warn you there are many loose floorboards."

The sergeant shook his head angrily and turned back to Bouboulina with a contemptuous sneer: "And what would *you* know about ships?"

Bouboulina pulled the decree out from her vest. "Perhaps you would like to review this," she said to him. It was the officer's turn to blanch when he read the *ferman* and saw the signature of the Minister of Finance, whom he had encountered some time ago and did not wish to see again. He handed it back to Bouboulina.

"Finish your business here quickly," he snarled to the three Greeks. "Soldiers, we will leave now. This appears to have been a false alarm." He grumbled under his breath, "Not the first time we've been roused in the middle of the night for a wild goose chase."

Bouboulina, Istianou, and the priest hardly dared to breathe until the heavy footfalls of the troops had faded into the distance. Finally, Father Constantinou opened the trap door and let the rest of the company back in.

"Well done!" said Kolokotronis to Bouboulina. "General Hypsilantis, please continue."

Hypsilantis smiled broadly and said, "We just proved that we can all work together. I have nothing more to say. Let us go forth and find new Society members who will further the cause of freedom."

Bouboulina raised her hand.

"Yes, Madame?" said Hypsilantis.

"I would like to join the *Philiki Eteria*."

A rustle of disapproval swept through the group: women had no role in such dangerous business.

"Why are you all muttering?" said Kolokotronis. "Don't you understand that this lady's courage and quick thinking saved the day?"

He turned to Bouboulina. "We did not meet you earlier. What is your name, Madame?"

"Lascarina Bouboulis."

The crowd fell silent. Even the Maniati stopped grumbling, for they were well aware that the Bouboulis firm was flourishing under the direction of Dimitri's widow. Still, *armatoloi* and sea captains alike stared stubbornly at the ground, not saying a word. Hypsilantis, however, knew better than any of the others how much Bouboulina could contribute to their Society; his uncle, the old statesman, had told him just before he was executed that he wanted the contract he signed with Bouboulis to be honored after his death. Thousands of gold ducats would soon be flowing from Odessa into Bouboulina's hands. Between that and her existing fortune, she would be well able to help the Greeks prepare for war. Clearly she was committed to Revolution. "I agree with General Kolokotronis," he said. "I am sure that the widow of Captain Bouboulis will contribute *immensely* to our cause."

Bouboulina came to the podium. "Gentlemen," she said in a calm, clear voice, "I am the daughter as well as the widow of men who loved freedom with all their souls. I know what I stand to lose if we do not succeed—my dear children are first in my thoughts. But they themselves would expect me to devote our family's fortune and our lives to the struggle for liberty. I'm here because I wanted to fight an attempt by the Ottomans to drive my family into servitude, and with the help of God, I won. Let me join you. And let me remind you that the women of Greece deserve as much as you to live in freedom."

The men fidgeted, but when Kolokotronis called for a vote, all raised their hands to approve Bouboulina's request for membership. And so, before leaving the house of her birth, Bouboulina placed her right hand on Father Constantinou's Bible and swore to devote her resources and her life to the quest for freedom.

IX

A Navy for Spetses

One week later, the *Capitanissa* and the *Elpida* were on their way home. Bouboulina sailed her namesake with first mate Harry, who had managed to get himself to Constantinople remarkably quickly on receiving her request for help. Captain Istianou had found able crews for both ships and was at the helm of the *Elpida*.

For much of the voyage, Bouboulina paced the deck, brooding.

Harry was more perplexed than usual. "Capitanissa," he said, "you should be rejoicing! It's nothing less than a miracle that you won your case in Constantinople and that we're all going home."

"Winds of change are blowing," said Bouboulina, "and I don't think Spetses is ready for them."

"Huh? What winds?" asked Harry.

"Revolution. Do you think we are ready to fight the Ottomans?"

"Why, I'd fight them this minute! Just let me at them!"

Bouboulina smiled. "Well then, I'll invite you to an important meeting when we get to Spetses. In the meantime, keep this under your hat." She saw the puzzled look in Harry's eyes. "Uh, don't tell anyone that we're planning a Revolution."

Finally, the pine-covered hills of Spetses appeared on the horizon. Word spread quickly from the harbor that the two ships were approaching. Even from a distance, Bouboulina could see the islanders gathering at the dock. The crowd parted to let Paraskevi, Lazarou, and Bouboulina's three children stand in front. Bouboulina swept them all into her embrace as soon as she disembarked. "You were right, Mama," she whispered to Paraskevi. "I was surprised to see how strong I can be."

The crowd led Bouboulina to the taverna, where she told them about the help she'd received from the Patriarch, Stroganov and the *Valide Sultan*. They were astonished that the Valide Nakshidil would even take notice of the Capitanissa and wondered, in their own hearts, if they themselves could fulfill the promise Bouboulina had made to her.

The family gathered around the Bouboulis dining table that evening—Paraskevi, Lazarou, Bouboulina's children, now all teenagers, and her half–brother, Nicholas. "The Ottoman Empire is rotten within," she said. "It will not be long 'til it crumbles."

"Let the first shots be fired here!" exclaimed her eldest son, Yiannis, who, with his curly black hair and deep brown eyes, was the image of his father.

Bouboulina frowned at him. "And then what?" she asked sternly. "The Turks would slaughter us. Can our ships face their men-of-war? No. We must prepare now to wage a long and hard fight. I am going to tell you about a secret society, a Society of Friends." She looked significantly at her children. "And it must remain secret. My life—and the lives of many others—depend on this." The children nodded.

Bouboulina described the *Philiki Eteria* and Hypsilantis's call for the recruitment of more members. A sad smile played around Paraskevi's lips. It seemed her family was destined to be forever entwined in this dangerous struggle for freedom. "And, of course," said Paraskevi, after Bouboulina had finished, "you refrained from joining this group of firebrands."

Bouboulina sheepishly shook her head. "No, as you guessed, I became the first woman to join the Society."

Lazarou said wistfully, "How I wish I were twenty years younger. What can Paraskevi and I do at our age? I can hardly pick up a musket."

"You both can still *think* quite well," said Bouboulina gently. "The young Hypsilantis, to his credit, is going to honor his uncle's promise to pay us for borrowing our ships—most likely because he knows we will invest that money in preparing for the Revolution. Soon we will have more ducats pouring into our coffers than we have ever seen. I will need your help to make sure it is well spent." Lazarou and Paraskevi nodded.

Bouboulina spoke to Yiannis: "I am inviting Spetses's most trustworthy captains and shipbuilders to a meeting, here, tomorrow evening. In the morning, I'll give you a list: you will need to find each one and ask him to come—nothing written, just say that we are holding a meeting for the benefit of Greece. And if he is willing, Captain Istianou should attend as well: he can help answer questions." Yiannis nodded. "I myself will invite Soula and Harry," she added.

"Lascarina," said Nicholas, "We can build ships well enough, but not the right kind. You've seen how much damage we suffer, even in battles with pirates. We need to build frigates and corvettes like the English are using now in their war against Napoleon, ships that can out-race and out-maneuver a man-of-war."

"That's obvious," said Bouboulina. "What do you propose to do?"

Nicholas grinned. "Where better to learn how to build these ships than in Britain's navy yards? I will somehow get myself into those yards. Within a year, I will be back with sketches."

"Uncle Nicholas," said Georgios, "I'd better help you practice your English." All laughed as they said their good nights.

At the next evening's meeting, Bouboulina and Captain Istianou described the Society's mission. They did not reveal the names of any other members, and they kept no notes of their discussion. Everyone understood just how dangerous it would be to join this Society. Still, the four captains and two shipbuilders who had been invited—along with Nicholas, Soula, Harry, Paraskevi, Lazarou, and Bouboulina's two sons—placed their hands on the large Bouboulis family Bible and took the oath of membership.

Bouboulina turned to her crestfallen daughter, Eleni: "When you are eighteen," she promised, "you too may join. Until then, I am glad that at least one member of my family does not live under the shadow of the noose."

After some intense tutoring from Georgios, Nicholas's English improved. He could read and understand the language far better than he could speak it, however. "If this is a problem," he thought, "I'll figure out some way around it when I get there." Within a month, he was bound for the shipyards of Harwich.

Next, Bouboulina travelled to Hydra. Captain Miaoulis had agreed to convene a meeting "for the benefit of Greece" in his mansion—a decision which required a good measure of courage since his mansion lay directly opposite the Ottoman fortress, in full view of the *Bey*.

Bouboulina stood before the wealthiest men of Hydra and explained how the *Philiki Eteria* was laying the groundwork for Revolution. Captain Delos, well known for his profitable trade in cotton, sipped his sherry and tried half-heartedly to keep a look of disdain from settling on his face. He delicately cleared his throat and interrupted: "Madame Bouboulis, we do admire your enthusiasm. *Certainly* we here on Hydra are no less patriotic than those who have joined this secret society. But look around you. We are not Spetsiotes or, worse yet, ruffians like the Maniati." A murmur of agreement rippled through the room. "*We* send our sons to the finest schools in England and clothe our daughters in the latest fashions from Paris. Surely you cannot expect us to sacrifice what we have built."

Several in the audience nodded their heads vigorously. After all, there was no doubt that their *Bey* would view this "Society of Friends" as a bunch of traitors. An uneasy silence settled over the room. Bouboulina gazed out one of the mansion's windows toward the Ottoman fortress. She thought of everything dear to her—her family, the school, her beautiful home and fine ships. Her face flushed with anger. How could this arrogant man think she had nothing to lose? Captain Miaoulis rose from his seat and strode up to her. All eyes followed him. "Capitanissa," he said, "get your Bible out so that I can take the oath." The men stared at him. "Why are you so surprised?" he asked, scowling. "The memory of the ill-fated Orloff rebellion—which our fathers refused to join—hangs over us, a cloud of shame. I, for one, will not finish my days under this shadow."

Captain Stenohori followed him: "I too will not see Hydra left out of *this* struggle," he said, "no matter *how* much my wife protests."

Captain Delos and two of his like-minded friends started to creep out of the drawing room. "Stop!" shouted Miaoulis. Delos turned. "If you *dare* breathe a word about the Society to anyone, you will answer to me! Do you understand?"

Delos's haughty expression vanished. "Yes," he answered meekly, and sidled out the door. Miaoulis and Stenohori took their oaths, and Bouboulina returned to Spetses.

Meanwhile, Nicholas threaded his way through countries of Europe that bore fresh scars of war. Napoleon's armies were in retreat, and spies lurked in every corner. He purchased passage to England on a ship that flew the Russian flag. Only after he reached the shipyards of Harwich did he realize that they were heavily guarded; none but Englishmen were allowed to work there. He found lodging in a damp, cold hovel near the yards and, after making an appearance at all the local pubs to try a new persona, presented himself as a homeless, mute man, desperate for work as a dockhand. It worked! Each day, while hauling heavy boards and barrels, he surreptitiously observed ship construction and made mental notes. Each night, though exhausted, he drew detailed plans by candlelight and hid them in the lining of his jacket. He returned to Spetses with his drawings in the spring of 1816. Soon after his arrival, the island's shipyard was buzzing. "No one else can build ships as fast or as well as the Spetsiotes," said the members of the *Philiki Eteria*. "Here will be born the navy of free Greece!"

One day, Bouboulina's sons approached her. Yiannis spoke first: "Mother, even the fastest corvettes and frigates will be of no use unless they are well-armed. Right now, among all the ships on Spetses, we have fewer cannons than are on one single

Ottoman man-of-war. And we do not have enough weapons or ammunition for our sailors—we need muskets, bayonets, pistols, gunpowder."

Bouboulina felt a chill run down her spine. She knew what they were going to propose.

"Arms of all kinds are easy to come by in Europe these days," said Georgios quietly—Georgios, her calm, thoughtful son, the one who most resembled Paraskevi. "Yiannis and I want to sail one of our ships to the Netherlands. We've learned of a few dealers there."

"And you want to smuggle weapons here," whispered Bouboulina.

"Yes," said Georgios steadily. "If we don't do this now, we will again be defeated."

Bouboulina remained silent for several minutes. Finally, she said, "The Turks had charged your father with smuggling weapons. If you are caught, you will not have a chance—they will hang you. They may torture you. Where will you say you are going, with a hold full of weapons? Have you thought of that?"

"Actually," said Georgios, "we have. In this war between France and England, Greek captains are running arms for both sides. We will say we are transporting the weapons to whatever country we are closest to at the time, and we will establish contacts who can back our story."

Her two sons gazed at her. Bouboulina knew she had no choice. "I give you my blessing," she finally said. "With every gun you bring here, let your father's death be avenged! Just know that I will live in terror of losing you."

Yiannis and Georgios were well aware that their smuggling jeopardized not only their own lives, but those of their entire crew, which, for this business, consisted only of Greeks from the Saronic Islands and the Peloponnesus. Finding and purchasing arms was not a problem; hiding them well enough to pass through customs inspections was. The weapons were usually buried in crates of grain or rolled in textiles. Gunpowder posed the greatest danger, as the brothers feared that one of their pipe-smoking sailors could accidentally blow their ship to pieces. If the sailors suspected that the heavy cargo they carried consisted of anything other than what was stamped on the crates, they said nothing. Once the contraband reached Spetses, it vanished—whisked away and hidden by members of the *Philiki Eteria* in cellars and in the caves once occupied by the Roma.

Fearsome brigs, corvettes and frigates soon emerged from the shipyard. First to be finished was Bouboulina's flagship, the *Agamemnon*, a double-decked frigate with eighteen gunports in its hull. Yiannis and Georgios beamed with pride when they saw those ports, for they knew that behind each would be a cannon they had carried, a cannon that would one day rain death on their enemy. Although Bouboulina's ship was named after

an ancient Greek king, its figurehead was a helmeted woman—
an Amazon.

Soon, ships commissioned by other captains were completed as well: the *Diomedes*, the *Themistocles* and the *Heracles*
kept proud company with the *Agamemnon*. Although the Ottoman tax collector, Mustafa, was now quite old, he could not
help but notice both the number and the size of the ships that
were rapidly filling the harbor.

The Spetsiotes worried that he would report all this activity to the *Bey* on Hydra. "What should we do with him?" asked
the shipyard owners. "Kill him?"

The islanders balked at the thought of murdering their
neighbor; the tax collector was no one's best friend, but neither
had he created undue hardship for anyone. "If we did that, the
Bey would realize that his reports are missing," pointed out one
captain. "Some of us can read their language, but no one can
write it."

"Take his family hostage?" suggested another.

Again, most villagers shuddered at the thought. "Even if
he did tell the *Bey*," they said, "could we kill his wives and children? They have lived beside us so many years."

"No," said Bouboulina. "No need for any blood to be shed
over this. Mustafa has spoken often of his wish to take his family back home to his village near Smyrna. We'll make it possible
for him to retire in style."

Bribery proved satisfactory to all. Mustafa, who had no
desire to see *his* neighbors hung, accepted their gold and their
assurance of safe passage to his village once the war broke out—
and submitted false reports to the *Bey* until then.

But the winter of 1820 did not find Bouboulina in good
spirits. Her splendid warships floated idly in the harbor. Other
members of the Society were equally discouraged. "What are

our leaders thinking?" they asked one another. "Can they not see that they are missing a perfect chance to begin the Revolution?" For in Epirus, Ali Pasha had finally launched an outright rebellion against his masters, aiming to set up his own sultanate. If the Revolution would only start, the Ottomans would have to fight on two fronts.

Bouboulina designed a Revolutionary banner for Spetses. She cut an eagle, the symbol of the Byzantine Empire, out of white cloth and sewed it on to a deep blue background. The eagle, representing Greece under Ottoman rule, sat, seemingly docile, with its wings folded. Clutched in its talons, however, were an anchor and a phoenix, symbols of its rebirth. On March 13, 1821, she hoisted the banner up the *Agamemnon's* highest mast and saluted. "May my country soon have a *national* flag," she prayed.

X

An Admiral for Spetses

One month later, the tavern keeper spied a brig in full sail, making a beeline for Spetses. "Hey, Pavlos," he called to the cook, "look out there! You ever seen a ship sailing so fast?"

"No! I wonder where she's from."

The tavern keeper squinted. "She's flying a white flag with—Holy Smoke!—with a blue cross!" For over 300 years, the Ottomans had forbidden any public display of the cross. "Quick!" cried the tavern keeper. "Fetch the Capitanissa."

Bouboulina raced down to the shore with her spyglass. By now, the speeding ship was close enough for her to decipher the motto on its flag. "*Eleftheria e Thanatos*," she read. Freedom or death—the motto of the Society of Friends!

The ship docked. Her captain strode to the village square where a crowd had gathered. "People of Spetses," he proclaimed, "I bring you good news! The Revolution has started. On the twenty-fifth of March, Bishop Germanos drafted our

Declaration of Independence and raised the Greek flag that you see on our ship. May it fly proudly over a united and free nation!"

The Spetsiotes cheered. "Tell us where the first shots were fired!"

"In Kalamata! When Petrobeys Mavromichaelis heard that the Turks were once again planning to invade Mani, he and his *armatoli* marched upon their garrison. In just two hours, the Turks surrendered!"

Bouboulina smiled. At the rate things had been going, the hot-blooded old warrior might well have feared that he would miss the Revolution.

The messenger continued, "Is Kyra Bouboulis here? I have a letter for her."

Bouboulina took the letter. It was from General Hypsilantis. The crowd fell silent as she read it aloud:

My dear Capitanissa and Friends, Command of the new Greek army has been awarded to Theodoros Kolokotronis. His valiant troops are now besieging the Ottoman fortress, the kastro, *at Nafplion. They are, however, running out of food and ammunition. Worse yet, our spies tell us that Sultan Mahmud is sending four ships-of-the-line to block the delivery of supplies to our troops, and to fire upon them. They left the* Porte *three days ago. I beseech you, brave captains of Spetses and Hydra, go immediately to the aid of our General. Only if you reach the Bay of Nafplion before the Turks can he continue the siege and capture the fort.*

Yours in the name of Freedom, Dimitri Hypsilantis

A noisy discussion erupted among the Spetsiote captains. Of course they would go, but who would lead them?

"Captain Stamos, you have ranged farther than any of us, even to the New World," said the captains.

"True," said Stamos, "but I have no head for strategy."

"Captain Lefkarou… "

"No," said Lefkarou firmly, shaking his head. "I am willing to fight to the end, but the thought of giving orders that could send my comrades to their deaths paralyzes me with fear."

All eyes came to rest on Bouboulina, who berated herself for not having thought of this earlier. "What were you thinking?" she wondered. "Does war consist only of gathering weapons?"

"Capitanissa," cried the captains together, "*you* were the one who rallied us to freedom! *You* brought the *Philiki Eteria* to Spetses! You *must* be our Admiral!"

Bouboulina gazed at the anxious faces about her. Like Captains Stamos and Lefkarou, she questioned her own nerve. But if someone did not step up soon, all their hard work would be for naught.

"Please," she prayed silently, "let me do the right thing."

"Do you pledge your support?" she asked the captains.

"Yes!" they roared in one voice.

"Then lead you I will!"

The crowd cheered.

"We have not a moment to lose," said Spetses's new Admiral. "Nafplion is a half day's sail from here. We must leave tonight. We will drop anchor just behind the promontory of the *kastro*. The Turks will not be able to see us there. They may reach Nafplion as early as tomorrow."

The captains raced to ready their ships. Every able-bodied man on Spetses joined a crew. Women and children hauled to the dock the arms and ammunition that had been hidden in the island's caves and cellars, along with plenty of grain for the famished Greek soldiers who were besieging the fort.

Bouboulina sat in her quarters on the *Agamemnon*, away from the commotion. She had to let Captain Miaoulis, who would surely head the fleet from Hydra, know that they were planning an ambush. She drafted a message and summoned her son Yiannis to sail as quickly as he could in their lightest corvette: "Yiannis, you must *fly* to Hydra; deliver this to Captain Miaoulis. If he agrees with our plan, his ships should join ours as we pass Hydra."

Suddenly, Bouboulina clapped her hand to her forehead. "The chain!" she cried. She had remembered that, across the entrance to Nafplion's deep harbor, the Turks had suspended a huge iron chain just under the surface of the water. They had borrowed this technique from the Byzantines, who had for centuries protected their harbor at Constantinople with such a device. The chain was fastened to stone towers on either side of the harbor. It could be raised and lowered only by an officer— in this case the leader of Nafplion's Ottoman garrison—who had keys to unlock the links that connected it to the towers. Quickly she scribbled on the message to Miaoulis, "I am asking General Kolokotronis to destroy the towers, so the chain will fall."

She looked up at Yiannis. "After Hydra, continue to Nafplion straight away. Take two barrels of gunpowder and tell the General that his troops need to blow up the chain towers."

"Yes, Mother," said Yiannis, as he raced off.

"And Yiannis," shouted Bouboulina, "Take four crates of rice—at least that will tide the troops over for this evening until the rest of our ships get there."

Yiannis, grinning, did an about-face and saluted Bouboulina. Bouboulina's heart burst with pride as she watched her daring son race to the corvette.

At sunset, eight warships of Spetses put to sea, four frigates, three brigs and one more corvette, with Bouboulina leading the way in the *Agamemnon*. As they passed Hydra, four more ships glided across the calm sea to join them, now twelve deadly shadows in the moonlight.

When they reached Nafplion, the acrid odor of gunpowder hung in the air, making Bouboulina cough. She knew that the gigantic chain now lay at the bottom of the deep harbor and that the ships could proceed to the small inlet behind the *kastro*. From the shore, Kolokotronis signaled. Her sailors rowed her over to speak with him. She was shocked to see the old warrior so thin and haggard.

"General," she cried, "I'll have our ships unload their grain tonight!"

"No," he said, "we can survive another day on what your son brought. Your mission now is to stop the men-of-war. After all, if they break through and start to fire on us, we won't be needing grain." He sniffed. "I just wish this gunpowder smoke would disappear. Best if the Ottoman Admiral does not guess the chain is down."

Each knew that sometime in the next day or two, an over-whelming force would descend upon them. "May God be with us," said Kolokotronis. Bouboulina nodded and returned to the *Agamemnon*. That evening, a steady breeze from the west did blow away the smoke.

Late in the afternoon of the next day, four hulking silhou-ettes, floating fortresses, appeared on the horizon. "My God," said Miaoulis, as he peered through his spyglass. "They sent their most powerful ships-of-the line, the ones that have three decks and carry over one hundred cannons!"

"It seems the Sultan intends to make short work of our Revolution," said Bouboulina.

Clearly, the Ottoman Admiral neither suspected that the chain was down nor spied the Greek ships hidden behind the *kastro*, or he would have advanced further into the harbor. Bouboulina sent six scouts off in a rowboat to gather more information. Hugging the shore, they rowed to the tip of the promontory and studied the maneuvers of the enemy ships. When they returned, their leader said, "They are positioning themselves so that most of their guns point seaward. Had we arrived this evening, they would have blown us out of the wa-ter. They are monsters but," he said with the hint of a smile, "so very *slow* and cumbersome."

"Yes," said Bouboulina, "our strategy will be built on that—their clumsiness." After conferring with Admiral Miaou-lis, she assembled all the captains. "Group yourselves into four squadrons. Each squadron will attack one of their ships," she said. "We will begin our bombardment from the landward side and then, as they turn, circle seaward and hit them again. Get as close as possible before you unleash your cannons. We know these waters far better than they do. We attack at sundown."

The captains and sailors from Spetses and Hydra readied their ships. Well did they know that failure would guarantee their own deaths and slavery for their wives and children. Those who could write drafted letters to their families. They bid their comrades' good luck and, if need be, farewell. Each one, silently or aloud, prayed for victory—and forgiveness.

At sunset, they cast off toward the harbor entrance. The Ottoman sailors, having just finished their meal, were looking forward to a calm night. There was absolutely nothing on the horizon. The old-fashioned behemoths were caught completely off guard. Before they could even lift anchor, the Greeks fell upon them, cannons blazing. Bouboulina's sailors roared and cheered as they attacked, in a way she had never heard—like some ferocious beast, she thought, as her own heart pounded.

The *Agamemnon* skirted the stern of its target and aimed its first volleys at the man-of-war's lee. Two cannonballs left gaping holes in the enemy's decks. They were close enough now for the *Agamemnon's* sailors to open fire with muskets and pistols and to hear the shrieks of sailors on the enemy ship. As she spied bloody corpses, some with limbs blown off, Bouboulina was overwhelmed by a wave of nausea. She broke into an icy sweat as she thought of Yiannis and Georgios, who were on the crew of the frigate commanded by Nicholas.

She walked to the *Agamemnon's* starboard deck, from which she could better survey the battle. The view was clouded by smoke billowing from the Ottoman ships. It seemed that the sleek Greek warships were running circles around the men-of-war. Here was the fruit of all their preparation!

Suddenly from port side came a terrible, splintering crash. The main mast of Captain Lefkarou's *Diomedes* had been struck by cannon fire from a man-of-war. It fell onto the deck, crushing everything below. Worse yet, the fire ignited the brig's powder magazine, and in a few moments, its stern was alight.

"Quick! Lifeboats to the *Diomedes*!" she cried.

A sailor manning one of the lifeboats shouted, "Capitanissa, what should we do with any Turks we find?"

Bouboulina looked to where he pointed and saw that, indeed, many Ottoman sailors were flailing about in the sea. "Rescue those who are alive. We'll disarm them and keep them in the hold until we can turn them over to the General." Ten enemy sailors were pulled from the water and taken below deck—of those, three were Greeks who had been impressed into the Ottoman navy.

Captain Lefkarou was weeping when he boarded the *Agamemnon*. "I saw two of my sailors crushed under the mast," he cried. "Their bodies were a bloody mess." He looked disconsolately at the wreck of the *Diomedes*. "Oh Admiral," he moaned, "to think I dreamed that my brave little brig could destroy their mighty flagship."

Bouboulina did not hear him. Through her spyglass, she watched the flaming wreck drift silently toward the flagship. The Turkish sailors were so busy defending their starboard side that they failed to notice its approach. She handed the telescope to the tearful captain. "Lefkarou," she said, "I think your *Diomedes* is about to…" A tremendous rushing noise drowned out the rest of her sentence. The wreck had crashed into the enemy's port. Within minutes, the Ottoman flagship was engulfed in flames.

The Admiral felt a chill run down her spine, for she knew that a page of ancient history had sprung to life. "Captain," she shouted, "do you remember the legends of the fireships?"

"Of course…" said Lefkarou, "we used them against the Persians, in ancient times."

"Yes! Barges set alight and left to drift toward the enemy fleet!" exclaimed Bouboulina. "We will use them again in *this* war."

"Impossible!" protested Lefkarou with a frown. "Think of the havoc they'd wreck if the wind changed and blew them back toward us."

"True," said Bouboulina thoughtfully, "but that would not happen if the fireships were manned for the first part of their course."

"*Manned* fireships? That's insane. Who would want to sail a burning boat?"

Bouboulina looked at him sharply. "Captain, have you thought of what will happen to *all* of us if we lose this war?"

This was not the time to ponder future strategy. The tide carried the charred hulk of the flagship swiftly out to sea. In its wake limped the other three Ottoman warships, their damaged hulls creaking and groaning. The Hydriote and Spetsiote captains found it almost impossible to resist the temptation to chase them. Admirals Miaoulis and Bouboulis had to remind them of their mission. "Sail straight to Nafplion," they ordered, "and deliver your supplies. Our soldiers are starving."

Bouboulina and Kolokotronis met again on the shore before the *kastro*. "Well," said the General with a broad smile, "we need those food supplies after all—the siege will continue."

"General," said Bouboulina, "I understand that we had to bring you ammunition, but why food? There are plenty of farms along this coast."

"The farmers would neither give nor sell us food."

"What a lot of traitors!"

"No," said the General. "They too pray for freedom. It's just that they are terrified. Remember, they live a stone's throw away from this province's biggest Ottoman fortress—they are an easy target for retribution, if we lose. For far less reason than our Revolution, the Turks have many times ravaged this coast."

"But this may be their one chance for freedom. Let us go and see if we can persuade them to join the cause." The Admiral and the General mounted a pair of horses and had just turned them toward the village of Myloi when Bouboulina's son Georgios galloped up to them.

"Mother! Mother!" he cried. "Wait!"

"What is wrong?" asked Bouboulina, dismounting when she saw her son's stricken face.

"It's Yiannis. He was shot during the battle. He didn't let on to anyone that he was so badly hurt, and went on fighting. He collapsed just as the sailor you sent to check on us came on board—we tried to find you. Mother," sobbed Georgios, "Yiannis is dead."

Bouboulina buried her face in her hands. A vision of Yiannis, laughing as he saluted her, flashed through her mind. "Why," she thought, "why did I send one of my sailors to Nicholas's ship? If I had only gone myself, I might have seen Yiannis one last time. If only..."

"I can't go on, General," she whispered.

Kolokotronis remained silent for a few moments. Finally he said, "You have lost your father, your husband, and now your oldest son to the cause of freedom. If *anyone* can convince the people of this region to help us, it is you."

"Mother," said Georgios quietly, tears still streaming down his face, "Yiannis would want you to go on."

"Will you come with me?" asked Bouboulina.

Georgios nodded. They rode to Myloi, each lost in thought.

The villagers started to flee when they saw the trio approaching. "Don't be afraid," Kolokotronis called out.

"We know who you and the lady are," said an old woman, "and we're ashamed that we did not give you the food you needed. But please try to understand that every day we live in terror of the Turks. They have taken so much from us, our land, our houses, our money...."

"I know," said Bouboulina softly. "They just took my son."

"My brother," murmured Georgios.

Bouboulina drew once more on some strength she did not know she possessed. "I can only tell you that if we hope to live without fear, we must, in this moment, be prepared to give whatever is asked of us."

The people of Myloi stood in silence, watching the General and his comrades leave. From that day forward, they supported the Revolution.

Bouboulina, Georgios, and the Spetsiote captains and crews returned to their island to grieve, to bury their dead—and to ready themselves for the next chapter in their struggle.

Fire!

I n February of 1822, the head of the rebel Ali Pasha was mounted on the gate of the Sultan's palace. The cunning Lion of Ioannina had himself at last fallen into a trap laid by Mahmud's henchmen. Now the Ottomans could turn their full attention to crushing the revolt of their bothersome Greek subjects. This became the mission of the Sultan's senior general, Dramali.

Week by week, Dramali marched farther west and south, toward the birthplace of the Revolution, the Peloponnesus. The Greeks raced to occupy the fortresses of the peninsula, for if the Peloponnesus fell, the Revolution was finished.

Day in and day out, the Greek leaders asked themselves one question: "How can we take the Rock?"

The Rock was the tiny island of Monemvasia, which rises almost perpendicularly out of the waters around the southern tip of the Peloponnesus. It had long been known that whoever controlled Monemvasia held the key to the Peloponnesus and the eastern Mediterranean Sea.

In medieval times, a vast stone fortress was built on the very crest of the Rock by French Crusaders and Byzantine Greeks. The stronghold had changed hands many times and was finally captured by the Ottoman Turks in 1715. Would-be conquerors could not attack the fortress head-on; they had to blockade the island and starve out its inhabitants.

For two months now, fleets from Hydra and Spetses had attempted to do just that. No supply ships had reached Monemvasia in weeks but, anticipating that their enemy would try this strategy, the Ottoman garrison had taken care to store enough food to last six months. Day after day, cannonballs from the fort rained down upon the Greek troops who were besieging it. Thousands of Turkish civilians had sought protection within the fort. They, as well as the Ottoman troops, were confident that their navy's men-of-war would soon appear and wipe out the Greek blockade.

Bouboulina's heart was breaking. Could it be that Yiannis had died in vain? Of what use were her splendid warships after all?

The worst was yet to come. A Greek spy brought dreadful news from Constantinople: "Murad-Ali will soon sail for Monemvasia," he said.

Murad-Ali was the newly appointed *Kaptan Pasha*, or Admiral, of the Ottoman navy. When he heard that the Greek fleets were gathered at Monemvasia, he hastened to the Sultan's chambers.

"Give me leave to attack," demanded Murad. "In one fell swoop, I shall wipe out those fools, those vermin."

"May I remind you," said Sultan Mahmud drily, "that those foolish vermin have cost us four ships-of-the-line?"

"Bah!" snorted Murad. "Forgive me, but the commanders my predecessor selected for the Nafplion expedition were weak. They panicked. Those who accompany me will have nerves of steel, like my own."

Sultan Mahmud looked skeptically at the *Kaptan Pasha*. He remembered that his mother had made no secret of her contempt for Murad—a stupid braggart, she called him. "How I wish my dear mother were still here," sighed the Sultan. Only a month earlier, Nakshidil had died—of a convulsive fever, said the harem physician. Mahmud had his doubts; to him, the death had looked suspiciously like poisoning.

"The *Valide Sultan* has earned her place in Paradise," said Murad grimly, barely able to hide his resentment as he remembered how often Nakshidil had barred his promotion. "Your devoted servant is always ready to do your bidding."

"Tell me why, *why* is this happening?" Mahmud tore at his hair. "Today, it's the Greeks who are rebelling. Tomorrow it will be the Bulgarians, the Arabs, and the Slavs. What do they want? To return to the days when they were a bunch of tribes?"

"Your Highness, they are ingrates. They do not appreciate the peace and prosperity that Ottoman rule has brought them. Let me teach the Greeks a lesson."

The Sultan sat in silence for some time. "Oh, very well," he finally said. "Attack."

When the Greek captains heard that twelve Ottoman warships were approaching, they abandoned the blockade and fled to the open sea. There they conferred.

"We cannot fight them," said Admiral Miaoulis. "By the grace of God, we defeated four of their men-of-war at Nafplion. Twelve will blast our entire navy to bits—and we will be fighting in more open waters where their immense size will not be such a disadvantage."

"But if we retreat now," said Bouboulina, "we will never capture the Rock."

"And if we fail to take the Rock, it is over," said Kanaris, a quiet captain who had brought his fleet from the distant island of Psara.

"We *must* fight here," said Bouboulina, "*and we must win.*"

"And how do you propose we do that?" asked Miaoulis, his voice laced with exasperation.

If ever there was a time to try a new tactic, thought Bouboulina, this was it. "We will use a weapon the Turks have never seen," she said.

"What's that?"

"Fireships. *Manned* fireships."

"My dear comrade," said Miaoulis, with some concern. "What are you raving about?"

Lefkarou interrupted excitedly. "No, she has a point! Listen to what happened at Nafplion." The other captains listened as Lefkarou told them how his burning frigate had destroyed the Ottoman flagship.

"But that was a matter of chance," said Miaoulis. "With just a small change in the wind, we might have had a disaster."

"Admiral Bouboulis proposed a solution," said Lefkarou. "At the time, I thought it was crazy, but now it looks like our only chance."

"Yes," said Bouboulina steadily, "we need not rely solely on the wind if we can control the direction of the fireship."

"You mean if we sail it?" asked Kanaris, who was acknowledged by all the Greeks, including Bouboulina, as the most brilliant and daring sailor in their ranks.

"Yes. At least to the point where we are sure it will crash into the target."

"Then, I gather, we abandon ship and row away like mad?"

"Of course," said Bouboulina. "And if the wind begins to blow steadfastly in the direction opposite our target, we can furl the sail and *row* toward it or douse the fuse and flee."

"The fireship has to lie low in the water," continued Kanaris. "Something like an old sloop that the Turks won't see approaching, something easy to row, if necessary."

"Yes."

"Hmm." The captain from Psara grinned. "I like it. The trick is to stay upwind of the enemy. I say we stand and fight."

The captains weighed their alternatives: dooming the Revolution to failure or staking their lives on this experiment. They chose the experiment and nodded their assent.

"Bravo!" said Kanaris. "I claim as my target the flagship of Murad-Ali."

"Captain Lefkarou," said Bouboulina, "how about we avenge your *Diomedes*?"

"Sounds good to me," said Lefkarou. "But let's stay out of Kanaris's way. We should go after the ship of the *Riala Bey*, the Rear Admiral."

Bouboulina, Lefkarou, and Kanaris set their crews to procuring two fishing sloops and converting them to fireships. Gunpowder, packed in a barrel, was placed at the prow of each fireship. And to the starboard side of the sloops were lashed the rowboats in which the fireship crews would escape.

All too quickly, the Ottoman squadron appeared on the horizon. The swift Greek ships stayed out of firing range. Murad-Ali was puzzled—and furious. Could the rebels be retreating?

No. The captains waited until the twelve men-of-war sailed downwind, further into the mouth of the bay. Then they fell upon their foe with a fury that stunned the *Kaptan Pasha*.

Bouboulina ordered three of her frigates to attack the port of the Rear Admiral's warship. As soon as they had a steady wind from the southeast, she and her crew of volunteers readied the fireship and beat toward the starboard side of the enemy ship. Not a single Turkish sailor noticed the approach of the low-lying sloop.

When they were thirty feet from the warship, Bouboulina shouted, "Light the fuse."

But within ten minutes, the wind shifted. The stretch of water between the fireship and the warship widened.

"Furl the sail!" cried Bouboulina.

One of the sailors reached for the bucket of water they had planned to use if they needed to douse the fuse.

"No!" shouted Bouboulina. "We can do this! All men to oars." They continued toward the *Riala Bey's* ship, rowing straight into the wind. Finally the distance between the fireship and the great hull of the warship narrowed to ten feet. Bouboulina saw that the flame on the fuse was now creeping across their deck.

"This will have to do," thought Bouboulina. "Alexandros, throw the hook," she shouted.

The strongest man on board grabbed a heavy, sharp iron hook and heaved it across the water. It sank into the warship's hull.

"Abandon ship now!" cried Bouboulina.

The crew cut their lifeboat free, scrambled in, and rowed furiously away from the warship.

Out of the corner of her eye, Bouboulina saw a few Turkish sailors racing toward the fireship—they had seen the flame on its deck. Too late. The flame ignited the gunpowder. A tremendous explosion ripped apart the rear half of the warship. Fire engulfed the splintering vessel. There was a lull in the fighting.

Greek and Turk alike watched dumbfounded as the *Riala Bey* and his mighty man-of-war slid to the bottom of the bay.

Safely back on the *Agamemnon*, Bouboulina surveyed the scene of battle. Captain Kanaris had been successful too. The blackened skeleton of Murad-Ali's flagship was floundering out to the open sea. Inspired now, the Greeks renewed their attack. Terror spread among the Ottoman captains. One by one, they followed in the wake of their Admiral, fearing that their enemies would harry them all the way back to Constantinople.

But this time, the Greeks did not forget their goal: take the Rock. The crews anchored their ships and reinforced the soldiers who were besieging the fortress. Turkish soldiers and civilians looked down at them in desperation, knowing their fate now was to be one of slow starvation.

XII

A Debt Remembered

For months the Ottoman navy sat in the harbor of Constantinople, licking its wounds. Perhaps the *Riala Bey* was fortunate to have gone down with his ship, for as soon as the *Kaptan Pasha*, Murad-Ali, set foot in Constantinople, he was seized by the Sultan's guards and beheaded. Sultan Mahmud, furious that he had been humiliated by his upstart subjects, wreaked vengeance on those Greeks who were closest to hand—the thousands who lived in the city—and on their Patriarch, Grigorius. Grigorius was hanged, his dead body dragged through the streets and then thrown into the Bosphorus. Bouboulina wept when she heard this, and wondered if Father Constantinou had been murdered as well.

Meanwhile, on Monemvasia, Turkish soldiers and civilians slowly starved as their food supplies dwindled. Kolokotronis's troops remained bivouacked on the cliffs below the fortress, keeping their siege. Day by day, the volley of cannonballs raining down on them diminished.

"They must be dying like flies in there," said Petrobeys Mavromichaelis.

"They are afraid to surrender," said Kolokotronis, "afraid they will be slaughtered."

"I hope we can prove ourselves better than that," responded Mavromichaelis.

"So few of their soldiers are left," said Kolokotronis. "It won't take more than you and a squadron of your men to capture the place. My troops and I, we'll head north to meet Dramali."

"Not me!" cried a chieftain named Lykos, as he crept out from behind a boulder where he had been eavesdropping. "My noble fighters and me, we'll avenge the blood of Patriarch Grigorius! I will spare no one—man, woman or child!"

Bouboulina happened to come upon the men at that moment and heard Lykos's words. "What do you know of the Patriarch?" she asked Lykos. "You think he would have wanted innocent people killed to avenge his death?"

"Oh, shut up, woman," snorted Lykos. "You don't belong here."

"Lykos," shouted Kolokotronis, "how dare you insult the Admiral! We would not be here without her." He saw that Mavromichaelis was unloosing his sword and, not wanting bloodshed at that very moment, growled to Lykos, "Just get out of here! Rest assured, your absence will not be noticed when we join battle with Dramali."

Lykos slunk off, and Mavromichalis returned his sword to its sheath. "It seems he's heard that the *pasha's* harem is trapped in there," he said, "with their jewels."

"I know," said Kolokotronis. "I hope Lykos and his scum don't disgrace us. Do whatever is necessary to control them." Mavromichaelis nodded, and they parted.

Bouboulina shuddered and remembered the words of the *Valide Sultan*, Nakshidil. Could she rescue at least the harem women and their children?

Only if she reached them before Lykos and his men. Through her spyglass, Bouboulina surveyed the walls of the fortress. There on the far north side, close to the stockade where the harem was supposedly sequestered, the walls had crumbled to the ground. This opening was guarded by several well-armed Ottoman sentries.

Finally, the day came when the Turks could hold out no longer. As soon as Bouboulina saw the first Greek troops storm the southern gate, she armed herself with a pistol and sword. "Please, God," she prayed, "don't make me use these against my own countrymen!"

Just as she had expected, the Ottoman sentries left their post at the wall near the stockade to fight the enemy troops pouring in from the south. Bouboulina climbed up the steep cliff and into the fortress.

Wasted fly-covered corpses were piled along the narrow alleys. Black rats swarmed over them. The handkerchief she held over her nose could not block the stench of rotting flesh. Bouboulina turned to flee. Then she remembered Lykos. Would this make *him* turn back? Of course not. She forced herself to continue to the stockade.

For several seconds she pounded at the door. "Let me in!" she finally shouted. "I've come to *help* you!"

"What could this be?" thought the harem women, who had resigned themselves to death. "A woman's voice?"

The *kadin*, the *pasha's* chief wife, opened the heavy door just a crack. "Who are you?" she asked in Greek.

"Lascarina Bouboulis. I've come to save you from the wrath of my comrades. Many years ago, the *Valide Sultan*,

Nakshidil, helped me. I promised her that one day I would repay my debt—in just this way."

The *kadin* had heard of the Capitanissa. The door opened. There in the stockade, the famished women sat huddled around their children, who lay on the floor listlessly. The *kadin* sank to her knees. "Lady," she said, "you are our only hope. We are half dead already. If you can change our dreadful fate, Allah will reward you."

The blood-curdling screams of Lykos's mob pierced through the sporadic cracks of gunfire. He was not far away.

"Get up! Quick, all of you, take your children. We can escape through a section of the wall that has crumbled and from there down to the water. If we can reach my ships, you will have safe passage."

Mothers scooped up toddlers who were too weak to run and followed Bouboulina. The *kadin* grabbed a small wooden trunk and hid it under her robe as she fled. Bouboulina helped them climb over the rubble of the wall and pointed them toward the *Agamemnon*. As she stooped to lift a small child who had stumbled, she glimpsed Lykos himself—and he saw her. "You hag!" he screamed. "Traitor! Give me those jewels or I'll kill you!"

Even with the child in her arms, Bouboulina ran faster than she ever had in her life. She caught up with the others at the dock. "Let down the gangplank!" she gasped to her astonished crew. "Take these women and children on board, quickly!"

The women could see their pursuers clearly now. Their swords and clothing were already dripping with blood, for they had found plenty of people to slaughter—children, women, old men. Suddenly, from the opposite direction, they heard the sound of running footsteps. Bouboulina's heart pounded. Were they trapped?

No. It was Anastasis Mavromichaelis, son of Petrobeys. "My lady," he cried, when he saw Bouboulina with the harem, "what is happening?" Bouboulina gestured toward Lykos's mob. As soon as he saw the blood-stained ruffians, Anastasis realized what they had done. A look of disgust and loathing crossed his face. He turned to Bouboulina and said, "I will protect you and these women until they are on board, and then my men and I will go after Lykos."

Bouboulina shook her head, for she saw that Lykos had disappeared as soon as he glimpsed Mavromichaelis. "Anastasis, that is what the General asked of your father: do 'whatever is necessary' to control the brutes. But look, they are already melting away—they will hide in the villages nearby, terrorizing our people as well as any Turks they come upon. Do your best, but we will need to find some better way to root these villains out from our midst."

The gangplank was now down. "*Kadin*," said Bouboulina, "one thing I must ask: if there are any Greek slaves in your harem who want to remain here, you must release them." The *kadin* nodded. Five Greek women came forward; they had been stolen from their families as young children and forced into slavery.

One spoke to Bouboulina: "We long to stay in our homeland, to find our families again, if they still live. But please, let us not fall into the hands of those terrible men who were chasing us!"

"Fear not," said Anastasis. "My men will escort you to a convent. There is one nearby. The nuns and priests will help you find your people."

The five women bowed to the *kadin* one last time. "Go with my blessing," she said.

As the remaining women boarded the *Agamemnon*, Bouboulina spoke with one of her captains. Returning the harem to Turkish soil would not be easy. By this time, the Revolution had progressed too far. If the women and children were brought to some Turkish village in Asia Minor, the captain, crew, and ship could be seized by the Ottomans. They decided that the *Agamemnon* should take its passengers to Odessa, where the French Embassy could handle their return to Constantinople. For the duration of the voyage, Bouboulina ordered, all were to receive at least three good meals a day.

Unbeknownst to Bouboulina, the *kadin* had stayed behind to listen to this conversation. Before she stepped onto the gangplank, she took the wooden chest out from her robe and handed it to Bouboulina.

"What's this?" said the Admiral.

"The jewels Lykos wanted," said the *kadin* over her shoulder as she made her way to the ship. "It's the least we can offer you."

"No," said Bouboulina, flustered. "I cannot accept these."

"Well," called the *kadin*, who was now on board the ship, "you have no choice." She smiled wanly.

Bouboulina peered into the box and gasped: rubies, sapphires, emeralds, pearls—a fortune.

"I will turn these over to our National Treasury," she shouted as the ship pulled away.

The *kadin* shrugged and waved.

XIII

Turning the Tide

After the victory at Monemvasia, all eyes turned north. There Kolokotronis was massing his troops to stop the advance of Dramali. The navy would have little to do during the next few months, as fighting between Greek and Ottoman armies would most likely take place far inland. The Greek captains returned to their islands to await further orders from General Hypsilantis.

As soon as she left Monemvasia, Bouboulina sailed to Nafplion, where a provisional Greek government had been established. There, she gave the *kadin's* jewels to the Secretary of the Treasury. He stared at them incredulously: "Good God!" he said. "The wife of an enemy combatant has financed a Revolution against her nation!"

Then Bouboulina was free to return to Spetses. She knew that her dear stepfather, Captain Lazarou, had died—peacefully, at home—while she was at Monemvasia. Up to his final days, he kept an eye on Bouboulina's expenditures for the war.

He knew that, like other captains from Spetses and Hydra, she had exhausted her fortune—building her ships, buying weapons, provisioning her sailors, providing for their families when they were injured or killed. Still, he and Paraskevi had themselves lived through even greater hardship and were confident that this time, all their sacrifices would be rewarded. Paraskevi moved into Bouboulina's house, and she and Eleni took in ten children who had been orphaned in the war. Bouboulina's once-grand home now resembled a shabby camp.

Bouboulina brought the school-age children together for two hours each afternoon. "Capitanissa," asked one of the girls, "why must we study now? We have so many tasks."

Bouboulina could see how frail and tired the child was and knew that, like the others, she worked long hours on the farm and in the kitchen. Still, she answered, "Times will not always be like this. When you are free, you will need to know how to read and write so that you can govern yourselves wisely."

When she was not teaching or working on her farm, Bouboulina walked to the port to survey her ships. She kept them in repair, as well as she was able, and dreamed of the day when they would again ply the seas, not with cannons and gunpowder, but with cargo from around the Mediterranean and the countries of Europe. Maybe someday she could even sail across the Atlantic to see the United States of America for herself—a new nation in a new world, whose founders had shaped a democratic government that inspired the Greeks themselves.

One winter day in 1825, as she watched from the *Agamemnon's* deck, a barque flying the banner of Hydra sailed into the harbor and docked. The man who stepped on shore was none other than General Kolokotronis.

"General!" cried Bouboulina in great alarm. "Why are you *here*? Has Dramali defeated us?"

"No, not yet," said Kolokotronis sadly. "Haven't you heard? I now live on Hydra."

"*What?*"

"New politicians have taken control in Nafplion, backed by European powers. They formed a government for free Greece." In response to Bouboulina's questioning gaze, Kolokotronis said drily, "Yes, I know, they're a little premature. Nevertheless," he continued, "they are pushing us to accept huge amounts of money from France and Britain, to let outsiders control our army and navy. I and several of the other Old Guard—especially Mavromichaelis—think that if we accept so much help from them now, the British and French will dictate the terms of peace between us and the Turks. Our arguments became so fierce that I feared we would start fighting amongst ourselves."

"*Now* I see how that rumor started—the rumor that I kept the jewels of the *pasha's* harem for myself," said Bouboulina bitterly. "Anyone who just takes a look at my house will see it is false—we have not exactly had money to spend lately. This new regime must be trying to discredit what you call the 'Old Guard'—all of *us.*" Kolokotronis nodded. He had heard this slander against Bouboulina; it ended only when the new National Treasurer issued an affidavit stating that the jewels had indeed reached the state coffers.

"Since ancient times," muttered Bouboulina, "we bicker amongst ourselves until our enemies reach our very doorstep. Not until then do we pull together." She focused her attention again on the General: "So, the politicos exiled you?"

"Actually, I volunteered to go myself. The threat of civil war broke my heart."

"This couldn't happen at a worse time. You are the only one who can defeat Dramali."

"It's even worse than that, Admiral. Another Ottoman general, Pasha Ibrahim, is marching in on us from the east."

"Mark my words, General: the politicians will soon be on their knees *begging* you to return."

"I hope so. But in the meantime, I intend to build myself a frigate. If I can't fight on land, I'll fight at sea. My son, Panos, said that he would help. He'll sail over from Hydra as often as necessary to oversee the construction of the ship."

For the first time in many months, Bouboulina laughed. Discouraged though he might be, the Old Man of the Mountains would never give up. The building of the General's ship cheered the Spetsiote captains and crews. Taking what time they could from their farming and fishing, they hewed pine trees and set the shipyard buzzing again.

Panos's visits to monitor progress on the frigate—and to pay the men now working as carpenters—seemed somewhat more frequent than needed. Bouboulina thought she detected a romance brewing between Panos and her daughter, Eleni, and her suspicions were confirmed when the couple announced their engagement. Although their wedding celebration was very modest, all Greeks took heart upon learning of it. Surely this union between two great Revolutionary families was a good omen.

Much as he would have liked, however, Kolokotronis could not attend the wedding. When they heard that the forces of Dramali and Ibrahim were massed in Thessaly, the terrified people of Nafplion stormed the Council chambers and demanded the General's return to the front. Just as Bouboulina had predicted, the politicians of the new regime were forced to admit that only the Old Man of the Mountains could save Greece.

The Spetsiotes cheered as Kolokotronis boarded his brand-new ship with a crew from their island and set sail for Nafplion. There he rallied Greece's dispirited troops and marched north to face the invading army. By May of 1825, the tide of defeat began to turn.

As she heard the bells of the old chapel peal for her daughter's wedding, Bouboulina wondered what the future held in store for this new couple. Of one thing she was certain: they and their children would be free.

Epilogue

The Revolution was to continue for several years. At first, other European governments hesitated to support a cause that threatened the existing political order. But in 1826, foreign aid began to pour in—thanks to the efforts of such Philhellenes, or friends of Greece, as the British poet Byron and the American doctor Howe.

Just as General Kolokotronis warns in this story, foreign leaders began to play a major role in running the war and, worse yet, in determining the terms of peace. In 1831, the Greeks accepted a peace treaty that had been drafted by England and France and that made Greece an independent monarchy under a king who would be selected from the ranks of European royalty. Civil war plagued the early years of the new nation's existence. Fighting finally ended in 1833, with the arrival of a new king, Otto, from Germany. Greece could now rebuild herself as a free nation.

Sadly, Lascarina Bouboulis did not live to enjoy her country's hard-won freedom. Her son, Georgios, fell in love with a Spetsiote woman whose family disapproved of the marriage. After the couple eloped, the young woman's angry clan stormed over to Bouboulina's house to search for her. As Bouboulina stepped onto the balcony to speak with them, someone in the crowd shot her. Lascarina Bouboulis died on May 22, 1825.

Historical Notes

Bouboulina is a folk heroine, surrounded by colorful legends. Researchers are shedding new light on her life and on the Greek Revolution. This novel departs from and rearranges confirmed facts mainly to better convey the spirit of the revolutionary times in which Bouboulina lived, but also to keep the length of the narrative manageable. These notes highlight points where departures from factual accounts of Bouboulina's life and Greek revolutionary history are *known* to have occurred, but they may not capture departures of which the author is not aware and they are not meant to comment on the accuracy of accounts that are accepted as factual.

Personal Life of Bouboulina and her Parents

Bouboulina's mother, Paraskevi, may have lived for a few years on Hydra after the death of her first husband, Stavrianos Pinotsis, before moving to Spetses. She is thought to have had seven children with her second husband, Lazarou, in addition to one child, Lascarina, with her first husband. Lascarina was born in Constantinople on May 11, 1771, while her mother was visiting her father, who had been imprisoned for his role in the unsuccessful Orloff rebellion against the Ottomans. Pinotsis died in prison. Paraskevi's brother, Ioannis, is a fictional character, and the account in the story about her parents and family likewise has no basis in fact.

Lascarina was actually married twice, first to Captain Dimitri Yiannouzas and then to Captain Dimitri Bouboulis. Both captains were killed in encounters with Barbary pirates. Lascarina had three children with Yiannouzas, the oldest of whom were her two sons Yiannis and Georgios, and three with Bouboulis; in addition, Bouboulis had three children from a previous marriage. Thus, she had nine children to support after Bouboulis's death. Bouboulina is said to have been a shrewd businesswoman who increased the considerable fortune she inherited from her husband. The account about the payment from Hypsilantis that appears in this novel is fictional.

The Ottoman government did try to confiscate Bouboulina's fortune, and it is thought that she met with Russian Ambassador Stroganov and the Valide Sultan Nakshidil in her efforts to retain it. The depiction in this book of a friendly relationship between Bouboulina and the Patriarch is a great departure from fact. Patriarch Grigorius had sided against her, and with her stepsons, in a family dispute and is thought to have excommunicated her. It is unlikely that Bouboulina became a member of the highly secretive Society of Friends, the *Philiki Eteria*, because the organization most likely would not have accepted women. Bouboulina did not run a secret school.

Military History

Bouboulina led a fleet of ships into battle in her flagship, the *Agamemnon*, which had as its figurehead a helmeted woman. Her ships took part in the sieges at Nafplion and Monemvasia.

Both ancient and Byzantine Greeks had used fireships against their enemies, but the idea of a *manned* fireship is said to have been born during the Greek Revolution. There is, however, no evidence that Bouboulina captained a fireship. Kanaris, a captain from Psara, made the most brilliant use of fireships, with his greatest feat being the sinking of the flagship of the Turkish Admiral Kara-Ali.

Bouboulina did rescue the harem of Hoursit Pasha. This occurred when the city of Tripolis fell to the Greeks, not at Monemvasia. Tragically, the women and children of the harem were among the few Turkish civilians who escaped from the city alive. Many thousands of Turkish residents of Tripolis were massacred. Both Greek and Turkish forces were guilty of terrible atrocities throughout the war. What happened to the harem jewels that Bouboulina supposedly received from the chief wife of the *pasha* remains uncertain. Shortly after her death, Bouboulina was awarded an honorary title, "Admiral of the Russian Navy," by Tsar Alexander I. Much later, in 2018, she was given the title "Rear Admiral" in the Greek Navy.

Entirely Fictional Characters

Several characters in this story are entirely fictional, including Soula; Ioannis; Stenohori and his family; first mate Harry; Chrysophilos; Father Constantinou; Beka; Alev; Ahmad; and some characters who appear in association with the Revolution of 1821 or the previous Orloff Rebellion, including Solaris, Stamos, Istianou, Lefkarou, Murad-Ali, Delos and Lykos.

Useful Words

acropolis – in ancient Greece, part of a city, usually fortified, built on a hill

aft – near or toward the stern of a ship

akse – silver coin used in the Ottoman Empire

Allah – Muslim name for God

Amazons – in Greek mythology, band of women warriors

armatoloi – Greek warriors in the War for Independence

Asia Minor – area that comprises most of modern-day Turkey

baklava – dessert common in Greece and the Middle East, made of phyllo, nuts and syrup

baptize – to make a child part of a Christian church, with a sacrament that involves immersing in or sprinkling with water; christen

Barba – Greek for 'uncle,' informal

Barbary Pirates – Muslim pirates who had their base in North Africa, in the area that is now Algeria

barque – sailing ship with three masts

basilica – an important church

beat – sailing with the wind using zigzag movements

bey – governor of a province in the Ottoman Empire

blood feud – a lengthy conflict between different clans or families

boom – horizontal pole extending from the mast, to which the base of a sail is attached

bow – front part of a ship

bowsprit – pole extending forward from a ship's bow

brig – two-masted ship, square-rigged or with sails set perpendicular to the keel or center line of the ship

brigantine – two-masted ship with a square-rigged front mast, i.e., with sails set perpendicular to the ship's center line, and two sails on the taller main mast, the upper one a gaff sail, or sail hoisted from a horizontal pole

Byzantine – related to the Byzantine Empire

Byzantine Empire – the Eastern half of the Roman Empire, founded in 330 A.D. by Roman Emperor Constantine I, which outlasted the fall of the western half by almost a thousand years; it was conquered by the Ottoman Turks in 1453 as the last Byzantine Emperor, Constantine XI, died on the ramparts of Constantinople without surrendering

caftan – a robe, tunic or loose-fitting dress worn in many areas of the Middle East

capitanissa – wife of a captain

chalice – cup for wine used in the sacrament of Communion in the Orthodox church

christen – to make a child part of a Christian church, with a sacrament that involves immersing in or sprinkling with water; baptize

concubine – a woman who lives with a man but whose status is lower than that of a wife

conscript – a person forced into an army or navy

corsair – a pirate, especially one operating from the coast of North Africa

corvette – a small warship with one tier of guns

dead run – sailing with the wind blowing from behind the boat

deck (of a ship) – flat area of a ship that covers the hull

dowry – property or money given by the bride's family to the groom on marriage

effendi – a title of respect in the Ottoman Empire

emir – title of a Muslim ruler

Epirus – region of northern Greece

ferman – a decree issued in the name of the Sultan

fireship – a ship, usually one old and no longer used, filled with gunpowder and other explosives, and sailed toward an enemy target; when its crew was sure it would crash into the target, they would set it on fire and row away from it

first mate – the officer who ranks just below the captain of a ship

flagship – ship that carries the commanding officer of a fleet of naval ships

fore-and-aft sails – sails that are set to line up with a ship's keel, or center line, not perpendicular to it

frigate – a warship

furl – to roll up

fustanella – white pleated kilt worn by Greek soldiers

garrison – troops assigned to stay in a town's fortress to defend it

gilded – covered with a thin layer of gold

Golden Horn – busy waterway that is part of the Bosphorus Strait

Grand Vizier – chief minister or head of government in any of many Islamic nations

gunport – an opening in a ship through which a gun is fired

gypsies – a group of people whose origins were in South Asia and who have a nomadic lifestyle; Roma

harem – part of a Muslim household reserved for women

heel (as a nautical term) – the tipping of a boat to one side, usually caused by wind blowing on the sails

hold (of a ship) – part of a ship where cargo is carried

hull (of a ship) – the watertight bottom of a ship, covered by a deck

icon – painting of a holy figure used as an aid to prayer in Byzantine and Eastern Orthodox churches

impressed (into military service) – the taking of men into an army or navy by force

Janissaries – elite troops in the Ottoman infantry who guarded the Sultan

jib – a triangular sail set in front of the most forward mast and running off a rope that supports the mast

kadin – chief wife of an Ottoman official

Kaptan Pasha – admiral of the Ottoman navy

kastro – Greek word for fortress

Kyra – Greek for "Mrs."

lanyards – ropes used to adjust the tension in a ship's rigging

lee – side away from the wind

man-of-war – powerful warship

mainsail – most important sail on a ship, especially the lowest sail on the mainmast

Mavromichaelis – last name of a famous Greek Revolutionary leader which literally means 'Black Michael'

minaret – tower on a mosque, or Islamic place of worship, from which the Muslim call to prayer is broadcast

Old Man of the Mountains – nickname for General Theodoros Kolokotronis

Orthodoxy – Eastern Orthodox Christianity

Ottoman – Turkish tribe, probably originating in Central Asia, which in 1453, under Sultan Mehmed II, captured Constantinople, the capital of the Byzantine Empire

Ottoman Empire – territory controlled by the Ottoman Turks which, at its height, included southeast Europe, western Asia and northern Africa

paidomazoma – forced recruitment of Christian boys into the Janissary force of the Ottoman army

Parthenon – ancient Greek temple on the Acropolis in Athens, dedicated to the goddess Athena

pasha – title of a high-ranking Turkish officer

Patriarch – spiritual leader of all Orthodox Christians

Patriarchate – the office and residence of the Patriarch

Philhellene – (Friend of Greece); non–Greek person who supports Greece

Philiki Eteria – a secret organization founded in 1814 in Odessa, which had as its mission the overthrow of the Ottoman rule of Greece (Society of Friends)

phyllo – very thin layers of dough used for making pastries and pies

port – the left side of a ship, when the ship is viewed from the front

Porte – administrative offices of Ottoman government

portico – a porch, usually consisting of a roof supported by columns

powder magazine – storage place for explosives and ammunition

prow – front part of a ship

Riala Bey – rear admiral or senior officer in the Ottoman navy

rigging – ropes used to support a ship's masts and to control sails

Roma – a group of people whose origins were in South Asia and who have a nomadic lifestyle; gypsies

Sacrament – in the Christian church, a ritual viewed as bestowing divine grace, such as baptism or Communion

Saronic Gulf – part of the Aegean Sea between Athens and the Peloponnesus which contains Spetses and Hydra

schooner – a ship with two or more masts, with the front mast smaller than the main mast and with lower masts rigged fore-and-aft, so that sails align with a ship's keel or center line, not perpendicular to it

ship-of-the-line – a sailing warship, designed to fire cannons in broadside, or from the ship's side

skufia – cap worn by Eastern Orthodox clergy

sloop – a sailboat with one mast, on which the sail is rigged fore-and-aft, and a jib

smuggle – to transport goods illegally across a country's border

Society of Friends – a secret organization founded in 1814 in Odessa, which had as its mission the overthrow of the Ottoman rule of Greece (Philiki Eteria)

spyglass – a small telescope

starboard – the right side of a ship, when the ship is viewed from the front

stem to stern – expression that means from front to back

stern (of a ship) – the back part of a ship

sudden jibe – sudden shifting of a fore-and-aft sail or boom from one side to the other

Sultan – a Muslim ruler; ruler of Ottoman Empire

Sultanate – area governed by a Sultan

tack – to turn the bow of a boat through the wind so that the direction of the wind shifts from one side of the boat to the other, allowing the boat to sail into the wind

tell-tale – piece of yarn or fabric tied to a sail or rigging which shows the direction of the wind and guides the sailor on how to adjust the sail

tribute – forced payments made by a conquered people to their ruler

Tsar – emperor of Russia

turban – a long length of fabric worn around a man's head or around a cap on the head

Turk – a person who is a member of any of several Central Asian tribes who speak Turkic languages

unfurl – to unroll

upwind – in a direction against the wind

Valide Sultan – mother of the ruling sultan of the Ottoman Empire

vassal – a country or ruler that is subordinate to another

Acknowledgements

I learned about Lascarina Bouboulis during my first visit to Spetses in 1984. Having just completed medical school, I was quite focused on starting my clinical training. Still, something about this dauntless heroine captured my attention: it was clear that she could be an inspiration to girls everywhere and that the Greek War for Independence was itself a trove of swashbuckling adventure stories. Although Bouboulina was recognized in Greece as a heroine of the Revolution, little was then published about her in English, other than in travelogues. My grandmother, Vassiliki Liarou Giannakopoulos, sat with me for hours on the porch of her home in Springfield, Ohio, helping me translate from Greek a fictionalized account of her life by Costas Bastias.

In 1986, I started writing the first version of my own historical novel for children, titling the manuscript *Bouboulina: The Adventures of a Lady Admiral*. Friends who read early drafts of the manuscript provided warm encouragement. As work and family obligations took over my time, however, I literally put the manuscript "on the shelf." Finally, when the pace of life slowed down momentarily, in 2021, I pulled down one of these early drafts—and realized just how kind my first reviewers had been: many parts of the novel were absolutely cringeworthy! Still, I remained convinced that Bouboulina deserved to be known in countries other than Greece. I rewrote her story, this time under its current title.

Many of those who read the manuscript in its earliest stages of unreadiness were friends who had graduated with me from Princeton. There were others as well, however, and unfortunately, I cannot begin to remember them all. This version of the story benefitted greatly from careful reading by Leslie Kipp, who had ample opportunity to use her skills as a copy editor. Janine Manheim and Bart Mallio constantly challenged me to "show, not tell." Frances Gretes helped me identify potential groups of readers. I am grateful that iconographer Dmitri Andreyev took on the illustration of this book; given the cooperation between Greeks and Russians in events leading to the Greek War for Independence and the prominence of Odessa in that history, it is exciting to see how Dmitri's style of iconographic illustration fits the story. The suggestions provided by Shahla Morris throughout the publication process made it all seem less daunting. Despite his busy schedule as priest at the Archdiocesan Cathedral of the Holy Trinity, Father Nikolas Karloutsos took the time to review the manuscript from a Greek Orthodox perspective. One friend, Jim Marketos, did not live to see the publication of this book; I think he would have realized that his own love for sailing is reflected in the story and that the values he embodied—scholarship, fairness, and kindness—are seen in the best of the characters.

Finally, I thank my daughter, Kristina Dinara, for reading and commenting on the manuscript and illustrations, and for her patience with me through multiple revisions.

Author *Katherine Kaye* first learned about Bouboulina during a visit to the Greek island of Spetses in 1984. She was certain that the story of this brave and resourceful woman, who dared to defy both the Ottoman rulers of her country and the conventions of her village society, could inspire young people the world over. Even in New York City, where Kaye resides with her daughter, girls face challenges as they set new paths for themselves.

Born in St. Petersburg, Russia, *Dmitri Andreyev* came to the United States in 1991 to study traditional iconography with his father, Vladislav Andreyev, master iconographer and founder of the Prosopon School of Iconology. While living in New York City, Dmitri established the Prosopon School New York City Studio. As an instructor of the school, Dmitri regularly leads iconography workshops around the country. He currently lives with his family in Brookfield, Vermont, where he works on commission and teaches private classes in his home studio.